Call of the Celts

BOOK ONE OF THE LOST HERITAGE TRILOGY

by Jenny Dee

Call of the Celts

Dedication

For My Nanny
The inspiration behind my own Celtic calling.
Your legacy and spirit will always live
on through me. This one's for you.

1

You live your whole life thinking you are one person, and in a single moment, your entire world changes. *Just. Like. That.*

This wasn't the first time I failed to recognize my reflection in the window overlooking Park Avenue; it happened many years ago, when I swore I'd never let anyone rattle my core again. But the secrets of others have a way of exposing more than random skeletons.

Without warning, foundations can crumble to reveal your own deepest repressed truths…the ones you can no longer run away from. This was one of those moments. For my family, and for me, life was about to take an unchartered detour.

"Ms. Rossi, the printer needs to know which copy we're going with," came the interrupting voice of my overworked assistant Derek. "Ms. Rossi?"

"Yes? Oh, sorry, Derek. Please come in."

I waved the tall, lanky millennial suit-wanna-be with glasses into my giant corner office with double walls of windows and gestured for him to sit down. I wasn't in the mood for this, impatiently tapping a pencil against the glass top desk to speed the conversation up.

"We need to get this over to Wentworths in the next hour or we're not going to make the deadline," he sheepishly repeated as he handed over the two different ads for review. My critical eye dismissed one version instantly and honed in on the fine-tuning needed for the other.

"Toss this one. I don't want to see it again. Make the font one and half sizes bigger on this one, move the text slightly to the left and for goodness' sake, please add a period to the end of that sentence," I uttered in distress. Why were good writers so hard to find?

"Tell Evelyn that if I have to correct her proofreading errors again, she'll be working in the mailroom instead."

"Oh—okay Ms. Rossi," he replied mechanically, glaring at me strangely before heading towards the door in an obvious attempt to escape my demonic wrath.

"I'm sorry, Derek," I called to him, catching myself in a weakened, unprofessional state of bitchiness. "Forget that last part. I'll speak with her later myself. Thank you for your help on this project." I managed a smile to let him know it was safe again to engage.

"Everything okay, boss?"

"Just one of those days," I shrugged off, knowing full well that if I let my emotions take the reign, I'd be the one working in the mailroom. And yet, I couldn't shake the heaviness of the last few days, as hard as I tried. So much mental clutter was taking up real estate in my mind.

The unexpected revelations, yet-to-be-uncovered mysteries and limitless questions infiltrated every cell of my brain, rendering me almost comatose in the everyday world. I grabbed my Dolce and Gabbana black coat, alerted Derek to just send the copy to the printer without my final review and left to pace the streets of New York.

In the noise, perhaps I could find some quiet away from my persistent thoughts.

How did I get here?

Growing up in suburban New York, we were a typical, and dare I say, boring family for modern-day standards. We had our struggles and challenges, as all families do, but no tales of tragedy, dysfunction or criminal records to claim. No hint of hidden secrets locked away in a dusty attic.

Just your ordinary troupe of five—a mom and dad who loved each other, along with three sisters, who even in their obvious diversity and distinction, had an unbreakable bond.

Our dad was a good man, loved by all who knew him. Oh yes, Joseph Rossi generously handed out compliments and was the ear you turned to in a crisis. He made genuine eye contact, opened doors and gave up his bus seat for the little old lady without hesitation.

A rare man indeed, if you ask me. I don't think they exist anymore—well, at least not in my generation.

He was a travel columnist for our local paper, the *WC Review*, and even though we could read his latest write-up in the paper, it was a whole different experience to gather around the family dinner table as he regaled his stories in dramatic detail.

I'd find myself hanging on his every word. Then I'd run right to my small little bedroom to take notes in my light pink wish journal about whether I would take that particular journey or not. I kept all my dream destinations recorded in there. I remember going back and forth with Daddy, imagining the different adventures I could have.

"What would it be like to run through the Australian Outback with a koala?"

"Or feel the spray of Iguazu Falls as you walked the canyon of Devil's Throat in Brazil?"

"Maybe I will fall in love under the Eiffel Tower's

night sky," I'd giggle as he kissed the golden curls on top of my head good night and wished me sweet dreams of newly explored territories.

Sigh. I wanted to be just like him when I grew up—a writer, a traveler, a dreamer. The reminder brought a brief smile back to my face before I shook off the juvenile fantasy. It had been quite a few years since I'd let myself reminisce so strongly.

I was blessed to have such an amazing father. He was so easy-going—and easy on the eyes. A twinkle in his soft browns caught the glance of every woman that passed by when he smiled and showed off those double dimples and perfectly straight pearly whites. Yet even with all that, he only had eyes for our mother.

And what a beauty she was—and is—in every way. Even though her days of pure blonde wavy locks have been joined by less-than-subtle strands of gray, and modest creases now dance around her delicate ocean eyes and sweetheart mouth, she still exhibits a youthful radiance and elegance.

I hope I will age as gracefully as she has, I thought to myself.

But it isn't her outer beauty that draws the attention of others—though it certainly doesn't hurt. She has a quiet power about her, a confidence that exists without arrogance. Natural, yet sophisticated. People listened when she spoke.

Literally. She used to be a college professor, and now enjoys giving lectures on the history of English literature. Her favorite time period, of course, was Elizabethan. In fact, we had a room in the house that doubled as her personal library and home office, filled to the brim with 16th century Renaissance novels and poetry compilations embedded into the cherry wood bookshelves.

Her favorite quote, which she playfully recited to our dad often, was from Elizabeth I herself: *"I do not want a husband who honours me as a queen, if he does not love me as a woman."* And how my father loved that woman.

It was interesting to see my parents together, actually—the adventuresome travel columnist and the bookworm homebody. But it worked. It really, really worked. They inspired each other, and that inspired us—even up until his untimely death three years ago.

Fuck you, cancer.

I'm Megan Rossi, eldest daughter of Joseph and Alissa. Many say I favor my mom, with my naturally curly flaxen locks, aquatic mermaid eyes, curvy features and natural confidence—though I tend to be a little more assertive and outgoing about it. I was undoubtedly the daughter blessed with my father's ambitious and adventurous spirit.

Travel has always been in my blood, and although I had a childhood passion for writing like Daddy, I found that to be too whimsical a career for me to be taken seriously.

Life quickly taught me that not all dreams are meant to be a reality, and that it was every woman for herself. Thank you, middle school bullies and a corrupt administration for teaching me early on about living in a man's world. That would be the last time someone would have the upper hand over me.

So, after excelling in advanced courses and graduating with honors from Columbia University, I opted to become an up-and-coming executive, eventually staking my claim in the world as Senior Vice President for an international advertising corporation.

And I am damn good, too, I smirked as I saw the approving text from the CEO ping my phone.

Excellent call, once again. We landed Wentworths.

I love the boldness of my job. Negotiating contracts and approving (or denying) the creative team's presentations gives me a rush like no drug in the world.

I savor the control—I won't lie. There's a certain kind of exhilaration in knowing I have the power to make or break deals, and that others look to me for guidance and leadership. The long hours and travel don't bother me. Neither does the money or the ability to live quite comfortably on the outskirts of Manhattan.

I never was a city girl, so it really is the best of both worlds—a quick metro commute to my high-powered job in a culturally iconic city, while living in the suburban community of Larchmont, New York.

"We're here, miss."

I let out a deep exhale as the rideshare I flagged down during my long, brisk city walk pulled up in front of my gorgeous two-bedroom luxury condominium. I couldn't wait to strip these stockings off my body and settle down into a deeply plush couch with a huge glass of Merlot.

Grateful for the break in mind chatter, I looked around my immaculate, well-decorated home. I loved every inch of it.

I am especially fond of my second-floor bedroom porch that overlooks the harbor and lush gardens of a nearby park. It's the perfect blend of rustic nature and the waterfront—picturesque and charming, but with all the access I need to city life.

Close enough to the family, but not too close.

Although I live alone, I have no regrets about that. I have the freedom to come and go as I please, and that suits me just fine. The men I've encountered in my life have been ruthless, narcissistic and well, let's just say, as committed to love affairs as a politician is to the truth. Disloyal bastards are everywhere.

Who needs a man, anyway? Aside from sex, they're pretty useless when it comes to relationships.

Oh, don't get me wrong—I don't hate men. I quite enjoy their company and the attributes they have to offer. I appreciate a good, solid wine and dine, with great conversation and even greater nightcaps.

I'm just smart enough to know that today's men don't have the same integrity and loyalty as my father and grandfathers and ancestors before them. No need to offer up my heart to be enjoyed and then discarded like the latest tech toy.

I don't have time for those kinds of distractions, anyway, I thought, as I poured myself a second glass. I fully intend to run this advertising empire one day, and that won't happen if I'm tied up in some little house-playing scenario.

I gave up my dolls in exchange for membership in the Junior Achievement network before puberty hit, which is why I knew I needed to get my act together and stop the mental madness. Thank goodness I was level-headed enough to pull off the Wentworths win today.

An incoming group text from my sister, Mia, broke my internal diatribe.

Just a little reminder that Sunday dinner will be at Meg's house this weekend.

Whatever would I do without a second mother? I muttered to myself. I knew she meant well, though, especially after our last dinner debacle. I simply texted back a thank you with a heart.

Our tradition is to rotate Sunday family dinners between our homes—Mia's was usually the best, as she was the culinarian of the family. Our other sister, Marissa, lived in the city, in a tiny and typically unkempt, true bachelorette artist's pad. When it's her turn to host, she recommends a cool little local dive she came across, which is just fine with us.

And when it's my turn to host, I order in. I still like the dazzle of setting an elegant table and coordinating theme dinners in my home—just without all the pain of having to cook. Marissa and I weren't born with the culinary gene like Mia, though Mar can be a bad-ass baker when she wants to be.

I chortled at how different we all were. From the outside, you would never know we were sisters.

Mia is Italian through and through, with her dark, milk chocolate waves and deep brown eyes. Over the years, she has embraced her much fuller curve potential, yet her beauty is undeniable. There is a gentle, kind look to her, with a soft spot for kids and animals that seemed to have passed me by.

After falling in love and marrying her high school sweetheart, Kevin Logan, they now have three kids, two dogs, a rabbit and I think an iguana. Or a newt. I don't know—some kind of weird reptile that their son, Stephen, wanted.

Sometimes I envy Mia's ability to find and live in love so freely. The Logans are the golden family of five, with their soccer mom van and picture-perfect Christmas cards every year.

But my observant nature sometimes captures that hidden glimpse of the wear and tear it takes on Mia as a stay-at-home mom (while Kevin works all kinds of abnormal cop hours), and I don't always feel like the grass is greener on her side.

I know. I have your color-coded dinner calendar on my wall.

In came the predictably sassy response from Marissa. She doesn't particularly love being spoken to as a child, either, but lacks the wherewithal to communicate that—or anything for that matter—tactfully.

As the youngest of us, she is truly an original character. I relentlessly teased her about being adopted when we were growing up but, she's indeed our blood—a blend of us all with long, straight ebony hair and contrasting eyes of azurite. Ugh, how I wished I had that dazzling and exotic combo of looks.

Tiny frame, great boobs—and she knows it, too. Skintight clothes are her preferred style of choice, and it works for her. Like a moth to a flame.

She has no shame in flaunting her beauty or using it to her advantage. She is single like me, but much more expressive in her entanglements. At least she attempted relationships—though she gets bored almost instantly.

As free-loving as our artistic little sister is, she is equally smart—she might as well be a Jeopardy contestant with all the knowledge stored up in that brain of hers. Her problem is that she hasn't found someone with the right combination to keep her both creatively and cerebrally stimulated at the same time. Or rather, she hasn't figured out she needs both in a partner. Differences aside, I do hope she finds that great love someday.

I sometimes miss the easier days of our youth. The five of us were tight growing up—made closer by the nearby presence of my mom's parents, our beloved Granny and Pops Mahoney, who lived only a few blocks away.

My Granny had an innate fire in her that was rare for her time, but she never let society stop her. She was among the few women in her generation to voluntarily get a job outside of the home as a bookkeeper for a bookstore—which undoubtedly opened my mother's eyes to her love of the written word. Any time a new book graced the shelves, a copy somehow found its way into Mom's hungry-for-more hands.

I like to think of myself as very much like Granny—a revolutionary, a trailblazer.

"Never let anyone stop you from following your heart," she'd always say. She was living proof that a woman could do anything she put her mind to.

But aside from all her fortitude, she could easily enthrall you with her life stories and solve the most hurt of hearts with her special cups of tea. Her kindness trumped her desires.

Although Pops was a warm and friendly guy, I wasn't as close to him as I was with Granny—but we loved each other nonetheless. We were all undoubtedly overcome with deep grief when he passed away during our early twenties from stroke complications. I remember the last few days he was incoherent, and some of the things he said to my mother just didn't seem to make much sense to us about her childhood.

Like, how meeting Granny and Mom was the best moment of his life. At the time, we brushed it off as ramblings of the stroke and didn't ask questions.

Little did we know there really was something we were missing; a clue that Pops was leaving behind. One that finally made sense after this past weekend.

That fateful Sunday, dinner was planned for Mia's house, to all our delight. When we were growing up, she was the one following Mom around in the kitchen, cooking up interesting dishes and claiming that one day, she would own a chain of upscale restaurants. (You can imagine where that dream went).

It's sad, really, because she has the makings of a truly talented chef. I'd rather hop over to her house for her latest taste test than frequent any of the high-class restaurants that lace the streets of New York. Well, most of the time, anyway.

When I pulled up to her adorable two-story stone and cedar Georgian Colonial, all seemed right with the world. It was as quaint as the Logans' immaculately landscaped front lawn with white and pink tiger lilies, red roses, deliciously smelling white jasmine and endless daffodils—courtesy of my talented younger sis.

Second only to cooking, gardening was a passion of Mia's. She could be found toiling away, humming to herself, finding peace in the dirt almost daily as the flower whisperer. A new piece popped up in the garden each time we visited to add to the floral rainbow among the red mulch clouds.

What made it even more special was finding a selection of her favorites of the week as a centerpiece for our dinner table. No one's home was more warm or welcoming than Mia's.

The inside was open and airy, with pine hardwood

flooring lacing the sophisticated, but noticeably lived-in dining and living rooms. She opted for earthy, yet vibrant colors, with expertly carved crown molding and handmade furniture. When Kevin wasn't busy fighting crime, my brother-in-law was one hell of a woodworker.

Mia's kitchen was her baby, though. With her love of all things food, it wasn't surprising that she put most of her time and energy into building her perfect piece of heaven.

All of the latest appliances in stainless steel sat upright among gorgeous Tuscan-style mosaic backsplashes, light-colored marble laminate countertops and terracotta tile floors. Pops of oranges, reds and greens danced around the walls with ceramic vases of fresh flowers and Italian art to complete the motif—along with vibrant lighting to keep the ambiance bright and cheery.

Her single window above the sink invited in the musical symphony of her hanging copper pots as the light breezes tangled in between them.

Walking into her home was always such an olfactory treat. We'd wager bets as we tried to figure out what she was making. By the smells of it, Indian was on the menu tonight.

"Smells fantastic. What's cooking?" I asked as I cheek-kissed my adorable little sister in her classic blue apron stained with the evening's dinner delight. Her hair thrown up in a messy bun and an oversized t-shirt and yoga pants meant that whatever she was making, she meant business.

"I thought I'd change things up and make some Chicken Tikka Masala, but with a few unusual twists, served up with roasted cauliflower rice and Naan bread," she beamed. "I think if I did it right, it should taste as delicious as it smells!"

"It always does," I smiled back at her, as I placed a few bottles of wine on the counter.

Oh, I could tell she was feeling creative—or sad. She became more adventurous in her meals when something was wrong. Out of all of us, she was the one who leaned toward emotional eating as her vice. I preferred wine. Marissa's was sex—pretty much for every emotion.

I wondered what was up with her. I made a mental note to pull her aside a little later to do some detective work. She could typically be a bit closed off about private matters, but persuasion is my job, after all. I'd break her like a Kit Kat bar.

My greeting was shortly followed by the dramatic arrival of Marissa. She should really pursue acting instead of art; she was a natural.

Even wearing a plain, tight black t-shirt and skinny jeans with knee-high black heeled boots and her hair tossed up with chopsticks, she was stunning—like she just walked out of the latest fashion magazine.

"Oh my God, the traffic was insane today! You'd think it was a freakin' holiday with all the people on the road. Jeez!"

"Well, did you bring them?" I asked, ignoring her self-indulgent fanfare as I gave her a quick hug—and then realized my answer. I grabbed the branded box from her hand and squealed. I loved having a sister who lived close enough to our favorite bakery in Little Italy. Nothing beats their mini chocolate covered cannoli!

"Now, now ladies…are you forgetting someone? Where are my hugs?" came the sweet voice from the living room.

"Sorry, Granny," I mumbled as I hung my head in

faux shame and then embraced her.

She smelled so good, like a subtle coconut-vanilla you'd find on a warm tropical island. Nearing eighty in a few short years, she wasn't walking as well as she used to these days; she recently started using a cane. But the strength behind her hugs was still as forceful and loving as always.

She hunched over slightly, with the plumpness of the most jovial of grandmas. Her all-white hair was short and wavy, and even with all her "wisdom wrinkles" (as she liked to call them), her turquoise eyes sparkled whenever she saw us.

"And how about for your mother?"

On cue, both Marissa and I ran over to sandwich hug Mom until she begged us to let her go. Her laughter was contagious—even the moody teenagers in the room who once resembled my sweet, ticklish nieces and nephew let out a chuckle.

With the Logan twins, Carly and Stephen, now thirteen and the eldest daughter, Brittany, edging towards fifteen, puberty (a natural trigger for automatic eye rolls) replaced their previous cherub-like attitudes. Every once in a while, they let down their guard and some childhood innocence slipped out…until they remembered to bury themselves back into their cellphones.

"Where's Kevin?" I asked causally. He was becoming increasingly absent from our traditional Sunday dinners. We understood why, though. He was recently promoted to detective, which meant extra hours over the last few months.

"Training. Again." Her tone was short and curt this time. Not her usual, sing-songy voice that let us know everything was perfect in her world. We knew that tone—

best to just drop it and not ask again, or probe further. At least not tonight. But I had uncovered the first clue in the Mia mystery.

Damn it, Kevin, what did you do now?

"Dinner's ready."

Breaking the ice as we sat down at the table, Mom told us about a new lecture opportunity coming up.

"It's really exciting! I've been asked to be part of an expert panel on Shakespearean interpretation at a symposium to be held at King's College. You know I never liked to travel like your father did, but I am intrigued about visiting London."

"Sounds wonderful, Mom! I think you will love it there. When is it?" I asked.

"In two weeks. I don't even know what to pack, or where to go, or what to see first!"

"Oh, you have to check out the National Portrait Gallery near Trafalgar Square! You'd absolutely love its Tudor collection, from what I hear," Marissa sighed dreamily. "Will you take pictures for me? One day I hope to save up enough money to tour all of the famous galleries throughout Europe."

"You will, dear. I can feel it," encouraged Granny. She always had faith in whatever our dreams were. "By the way, have you been working on any of your own art lately?" she nudged.

She's about the only one in our family who could get away with blatant nosiness and still be adored for it.

"Well, I, um, have been a little busy and distracted. I had to pick up another gig waitressing during the day since Tony moved out."

"Wait, what?" I turned my head. Tony was her latest roomie. They were friends who decided that sharing a place and expenses would help them both save up money while working towards their prospective dreams.

"It just wasn't working out," she said nonchalantly. "It's okay, though. He was too much of a slob anyway."

Awkward silence filled the air. "You slept with him, didn't you?"

"Megan!" Mia shot me a hard glance from across the table, only because her leg couldn't reach to kick me.

"What? I'm just saying what everyone was thinking. Look, Mar, the whole point of moving in with a platonic friend is for it to stay platonic. You know that, right?"

But I don't think she did. Marissa was known for her romantic dabbling and musical chair roommates because of it. A bartender by trade, she was still struggling to make her art dreams a reality but never could swing the rent on her own. She wanted to become a modern-day Francisco de Goya (her favorite artist), and even though she's had little success so far, she was determined to catch a break one day.

Which may explain her attempts to form relationships with men of power (sometimes women—she didn't discriminate) or even fellow artists. It's not that she intended to use anyone; not at all. She was just drawn to kindred spirits and figured if she was attracted to those who might help her out as well, then what's the harm?

But they never held her interest for long. Tony was just the next victim on her list.

Before the conversation could intensify with a snarled rebuttal, the doorbell rang.

"You expecting anyone, honey?" Mom wondered aloud.

"No," Mia said, as she cautiously rose from the table to peek through the peephole.

She had become a little more nervous than usual these days, adjusting to being alone frequently with Kevin's new position taking him away from the house so often.

"Who is it?"

"My name is Joshua Perkins, ma'am, of the Sanderson Law Firm. I need to speak with Alissa Rossi and her daughters on a legal matter. I was told I could find them here."

Confused yet intrigued, we all made our way towards the door as Mia carefully opened it to reveal an incredibly handsome, well-dressed man holding a stylish briefcase. He was tall in stature with a well-defined build.

Dirty blonde, Ivy-League cut hair. Green eyes. Small, thin lips. A little on the pasty-skinned side. Blue micro-striped twill Giorgio Armani suit, Fendi briefcase, Rolex watch—and are those Berlutis on his feet? Damn, this guy reeked of money.

"Please, come in," Mia invited, as she fumbled with her hair and clothes, feeling embarrassingly underdressed in the moment. Not quite ready to fully let him inside, we all formed a small horseshoe in the foyer like a fierce barrier of protection waiting to see what this man wanted from us on a random Sunday evening.

"I'm sorry to disturb you at home, and at such a late hour," he started.

"How can we help you, Mr. Perkins?" Oh boy. Fluttering eyelashes as she asked. Was there seriously no one that Marissa wouldn't flirt with? And, of course, he returned the flirtation with his own coy lift of his lips that he tried to professionally suppress.

He quickly regained his composure with a clearing of his throat to deliver his news.

"I'm here with deepest condolences to inform you of

your grandfather's passing, and to make arrangements for the reading of his will."

"Wait—what? I don't understand," I interjected. "What are you talking about? Our Pops died over ten years ago, and our dad's father died before we were even born. What is this all about?"

"I'm sorry for the confusion, Ms. Rossi. I'm here about your mother's *biological* father. Leigh Marino. He recently passed away, about ten days ago."

2

S tunned, the room jolted into darkness like a rural neighborhood after a power outage.

Yet even through the shockwave, I observed the guilty glance exchanged briefly between my mother and grandmother before they joined us in mock surprise—just enough to know that the assumed con man standing in front of us might actually be speaking a hint of truth.

A few awkward moments passed before Mia spoke up.

"I'm sorry, you seem to have caught us off guard. Please, come in and sit down, Mr. Perkins." As she guided all of us towards the living room, she continued to speak with composure. Graceful like Mom. "May I offer you something to drink?"

"No, thank you. I seem to have interrupted your dinner. I'm sorry. I will be brief."

Intuiting the complicated nature of the meeting, Mia nudged her children up to their rooms to give us some privacy. With a few of those famous eye rolls and some grunts, they begrudgingly moved up the stairs—though I'm pretty sure they didn't mind being excused from the adult drama that was about to ensue.

All of us now settled on her family-worn, but irresistibly comfortable plush beige couches in front of a lit stone-framed fireplace, the questions and comments came flooding in.

"Are you sure you have the right family?"

"What do you mean, *biological* grandfather?"

"Is this some kind of joke?"

"Whoa, whoa, ladies—don't shoot the messenger." Joshua Perkins became increasingly uncomfortable being the brunt of the mayhem, loosening his light blue Gucci silk tie in an effort to breathe.

"I'm sorry, Mr. Perkins," I began, trying to set the tone for a more civilized conversation. "As you can see, this all comes as quite a shock to us. We never heard of this Leigh Marino before, so perhaps you can help us understand what is going on here."

Even though I was suspicious of the man sitting in front of us, I was willing to hear him out, even if it meant learning something that clearly unsettled my mother and grandmother.

"Forgive me, Ms. Rossi."

"Call me Megan," I insisted.

"Okay, Megan. I apologize for my bluntness about your grandfather. I didn't consider that any of you would not be aware of his existence. I can certainly understand how this must come as a surprise to you—to all of you."

"Of course we're surprised. You're fucking lying and I'd love to know why." Leave it to Marissa to explode like that accidentally-lit firecracker. "Who are you and what do you really want with our family?"

She leaned in closer to him, almost all up in his face, as if to intimidate him. As much as her eyes could seduce, they could stab with a thousand knives.

"Marissa, please," begged our mother, with tears welling. "Let him speak."

She turned back to Mr. Perkins with nervous

attentiveness. And there it was. The validation that what this random stranger just revealed to us could be the truth—or at least, the beginning of it. "Please, go on."

"Thank you. Again, I'm so sorry to be the bearer of bad news." He started to shift even more uneasily in his seat, wishing to be anywhere but here in this moment.

"As I understand it, Leigh Marino is your biological father," and then turning to us, "and your biological grandfather. He passed away almost two weeks ago after a long battle with pancreatic cancer."

Fuck cancer. Again. Another one of its unnecessary victims, and I didn't even know the man.

"He was diagnosed three years ago and underwent extensive treatment, but over the last two months, his health was failing fast. During that time, he was putting his affairs in order, but remained obscure about settling some of his final wishes."

On that note, he opened his briefcase to reveal a rather large, sealed, official-looking white envelope. He had beautiful hands, I noticed. Nails well groomed, too. Soft hands that would probably feel great on my body.

I shook the imagined sensation off, returning my attention to the matter at hand.

"He insisted that aside from his official will, this envelope of sealed letters was not to be delivered nor opened until his death, and not until after the official reading of his will."

He respectfully paused for us to digest just a little of what he was telling us before continuing.

"This envelope was released from his personal safety box a few days ago, with specific instructions that I was to personally find you all and schedule a reading. I am required to be in the audience of Alissa Rossi, her three daughters and Lillith Mahoney, if she is still alive."

"Oh, I am very much still alive." And in a very uncharacteristic, yet still composed tone, she uttered, "We're all here. Let's hear what the son-of-a-bitch had to say."

"Mama. May I have a moment? In the kitchen?" Mom turned to us apologetically with obvious fear and worry in her baby blues as she helped our grandmother up off of the couch. "Excuse us."

Looking at each other questioningly, we reluctantly allowed them their privacy. Although I can't read my sisters' minds, I know them well enough that I can imagine they are feeling just as betrayed and pissed off as I am.

Well, at least Marissa is. In that mind of hers, Mia was probably rationalizing it all out and figuring out a way to play peacekeeper. Typical Pollyanna.

Well, whatever they had to say, they should be able to say it to us. After all, they seem to not be surprised and we are owed some answers. I'll give them five minutes before I bust in there...

But I couldn't wait that long. I tiptoed towards the kitchen to listen in on their secret conversation. Mia tried to dissuade me, but with a single authoritative look, I hushed her immediately and held up my hand to stop Marissa from joining me, to her pissed off chagrin.

"Mama, don't you think we should speak in private with the girls before allowing this to go any further?"

"I don't know. Maybe you are right." A quick beat passed as Granny looked up at Mom. "What have I done? How could this have happened? Your father and I forged an agreement long ago to never, ever speak of this. How could he blindside me like this?"

"I'm not sure, Mama. But I think we owe it to those girls out there to tell them the truth before we get into the reading of his will. I can see the pain in their eyes. The betrayal. All they have known is about to be turned upside down."

"I'm so sorry, Alissa. So, so sorry. I should not have forced you into silence all those years ago. I only hope this secret has not cost you your daughters. Or me my granddaughters." She took Mom's hands and looked sorrowfully into her eyes. "What have I done to our family?"

I saw Mom look back lovingly at her. "So, we might have made a mistake keeping this from them. We had our reasons at the time, and they were good ones. But we will fix this. We are strong and we can get through anything together."

She squeezed Granny's hands softly. "Now, let's go back in there. We have some explaining to do."

I quickly ran back to sit on the couch as if I had never moved. Hand in hand, they walked into the deadly quiet and heavily emotional room. My mother was the one to break the silence.

"You'll have to excuse us, Mr. Perkins. We need some time to discuss this as a family. If you can leave us your number, we will be in touch to arrange another time for the will reading."

"Of course." Reaching into his inside jacket pocket, he pulled out his fancy business card and handed it to my grandmother, who was standing right next to him.

An odd look came across Granny's face as she scanned the card. "Perkins." Her eyes widened with a surprised recognition as she looked up at the young man in front of her. "Any relation to Julia Perkins?"

"Yes, ma'am," he barely got out, shifting anxiously as five strong women stared him down. "She's my, um, great-aunt."

"Interesting," she replied, not removing her eyes from his.

Then once again, the room filled with a dreaded pause (like one from a horror movie) before he smartly wished us a good evening and exited in self-preservation mode.

After the well-to-do lawyer left, the ambiance became even more intense. We all had something to say yet were too faint-hearted to start. I mean, where do you begin a conversation like this?

So, Pops wasn't our real Pops? Who was this Leigh Marino guy, and why have we never heard of him or met him? Obviously, Granny knew about this, but how long did Mom know about it? Why was it such a big secret? And what does he want with us now?

"Will one of you please explain what in the hell is going on here and how come we didn't know about some secret grandfather?" Marissa demanded angrily.

"Seriously, Marissa? Cool your jets and let them explain," I snapped back.

"Why are *you* so calm about this? You are usually a hothead, too. Or did you already know about this? Being the privileged eldest, I wouldn't be surprised."

"I don't know a damn thing. But if you shut your trap, maybe we can find out."

"Don't talk to me like I'm one of your work minions, Meg."

"GIRLS."

Granny had a way of raising her voice that elicited complete silence, and she didn't use it often. She may be old—but she was not fragile.

"Attacking each other is not going to help anything. You have a right to be angry with your mother and I, but not with each other."

She took each of our right hands and brought them together in a ceremonial-like hand holding.

"No matter what you learn tonight, promise me here and now that no matter what happens, that you will always stick together and not let this or anything or anyone come between you."

We nodded in silence.

"PROMISE ME," she ordered like a drill sergeant.

We all looked up at each other, nodded and in unison declared, "We promise."

"Good." Granny then looked over at my mother, who was a mixed bag of sadness, heartache and guilt—a limp little ragdoll of a child wishing for her favorite stuffed animal. If she could curl up in the corner with her legs pulled up to her chest right now, she would.

"Alissa, would you mind if I explained it all? It's about time I get this burden off my chest."

"Of course," Mom sighed gratefully with obvious relief and an almost instantaneous return to her normal regal composure.

Grateful for the support, Granny closed her eyes and took three deep, deep breaths. On her last exhale, I thought I saw the suppression of a tiny drop near her saddened eyes, no doubt only the beginning of a pain she was about to relive in the name of telling the truth.

"All I ask of you is that you hear me out first. I know full well that you have plenty of questions, and I promise I will be honest and answer them all. But I need to tell you all of this in my own way, and I ask for your patience and understanding as I clear everything up."

I reached out to stroke her back gently. I couldn't help but go from angry to unconditionally sympathetic towards her. For her to keep something of this magnitude a secret, it must have been sincerely painful.

"Of course, Granny. Take your time." I looked at my sisters and delivered another silent command as the eldest. "We promise to listen without judgment." Mia and Marissa bowed their head in quiet agreement.

"Where to begin?" My heart was already breaking as she looked wistfully into the distance, reaching for that elusive butterfly that was flying away.

"Even when I was young, I knew I was different from other girls my age. They were all playing dolls and house and cheerfully helping their mothers clean and learning how to cook and sew, and all the things a *proper* young lady should be learning to do in order to become a good, dutiful wife.

"But for whatever reason, that just wasn't for me. I'd watch my father come home and continue working by candlelight. He was such a kind man—not unlike your own father. Even though it was not supposed to be encouraged, he indulged my questions about his work and occasionally would take the time to teach me skills that typically only boys were taught.

"I remember him telling me, 'Lillith, never let anyone put out your fire or deter you from your dreams. Society does not define who you are. You can be anyone you want to be.'"

The memory brought a warm smile to her heart. I could see her looking back to a time when she was bouncing on his fatherly knee, transforming easily from manly provider to a child's pony. No doubt, daddy's little girl. Just like me.

"As you know, my father died just a few short weeks before I completed school. But his words never left my heart. Against my mother's wishes, I pursued various jobs—any jobs that were willing to hire a woman at the time.

"In my heart of hearts, I yearned to be one of the few to go to college and major in criminal justice. But alas, coming from a family with little means to begin with, and with my mother left without a husband in those times, that dream was an impossibility.

"I eventually earned a reputation as a hard worker with a good work ethic—and astonished the men in the jobs I worked for with my intelligence, confidence and skills. Daddy taught me well. It was when I took my first bookkeeping job at an art gallery that I met Leigh Marino."

She took a moment for an aside. "Actually, I wasn't bookkeeping at that moment. The gallery was having an event and needed waitresses, so of course the women of the company were expected to help fill that role." She rolled her eyes gently before brushing off the sexist experience and continuing.

"I remember the moment we met clear as day. I was passing around flutes of champagne to these hoity-toity art snobs, when he accidentally took a step backward into me and my tray went flying.

"I was so angry at first—how dare he not look where he was going; he ruined my new white shirt! But then he stunned me when he just laughed as he excused himself for his clumsiness.

"It wasn't the typical condescending man's laugh I was used to, though. No, it was more of a nervous, amused, yet intrigued kind of laugh. He helped me clean up the mess, profusely apologizing while I remained irate and spoiled.

"He handed me his classy, monogrammed handkerchief and the instant our hands touched, I knew my life would never be the same." There was that smile, the one that persuaded you to believe in true love at first sight…dare her it wasn't possible.

"When I looked up, I saw him. Truly saw him. Tall— elegantly tall in stature, with short, dark wavy hair and life-shattering aqua blue eyes that could melt an iceberg in an instant. The exoticness of the Mediterranean with the softness of an Irishman. Yes, a fascinating combination," she recalled to herself.

She looked at Marissa. "You look just like him, dear. I see him in you more and more every day," she reflected as she ran a wrinkled finger down Mar's cheek with love.

"His smile was broad and warm and felt like home. His hands were smooth and manly—but not a rough manly. A strong manly."

Granny paused for a moment, lost in the reverie. You could see her light up with the thought of love—and just as quickly as it came, it left her face.

"After that night, he began to court me. It was doomed from the beginning, though. He came from an affluent family with generations of royalty and prestige, and I was the lucky product of simple Irish immigrants who came through Ellis Island and settled in Brooklyn to find a better life for themselves.

"His family would never approve of me—and in fact, he was already betrothed to another heiress of great fortune. Money must stay with money, after all," she said bitterly.

"But—my Leigh was not like that. Not at first, anyway. He tried to fight his family and the betrothal. He asked me to run away with him, to start a new life together. He didn't care that he would be disowned. It was all so romantic and tempting. But I couldn't ask him to turn his back on his family, not even in the name of love.

"One night, he left me no choice. He packed what little possessions he could bring with him to fetch some money until he could secure a job of his own. He had already left his family and was no longer welcomed back. If I were to deny him, I'd leave him with nothing but a broken heart and no family.

"How could I turn my back on the man who lost everything to love me?

"We didn't stray too far—just enough to settle a few hours north of the city, where we would be away from the influences of his family and the high cost of living. We married the instant we found our home and declared our everlasting love. It was a beautiful life.

"He was able to find employment with a local law firm and I worked in the library. We'd both go to work during the day and come home and make endless love every night. It took quite a while, but a few years after we were married, I finally became pregnant with our Alissa. We were ecstatic and happier than any couple I had ever known. It was a fairy tale come true."

Sigh. I couldn't help but be caught up in the romance of it all, noting Mia and Marissa had the same dreamy looks upon their faces and a conflicted joy in my mother's, as I assume she hadn't heard this version of their love story all that often.

"But it was not meant to last." Deep sorrow and muffled moans erased the sentimentality in the air.

"When Alissa was five years old, Leigh received an urgent message that his father was ill and calling him home. I never thought they would have been able to track us down after all those years—or care to do so. I remember him feeling distraught over what to do.

"Ever the optimist, he thought that perhaps in his dying years, his father had come to accept his decision to love some peasant woman, as that man called me, and welcome all of us into the family.

"He wanted to rebuild his relationship with his father and perhaps reclaim his rightful fortune—which he declared would be used to send me to college to fulfill my dream of becoming a criminal justice lawyer. He said he wanted to build an even more magical life for the three of us, and even try to have more babies.

"I believed him. I believed his foolish fantasies and lovingly kissed him goodbye as I promised to watch over our precious daughter until his return. He vowed he would come home soon.

"He wrote us daily in the beginning, filling us in on how his father was so pleased to see him, but he was so ill that he had to take part in his care. He firmly believed that in doing so, he was securing our future and his place once again in the family. He wanted it all.

"But then the letters dwindled from daily to weekly and then monthly, with claims that caring for his father was exhausting beyond belief. Weeks turned into months, and those soon turned into a year. Alissa was then six and I was left, without a husband, to manage a house and family on my own. The money he sent to support us diminished along with the letters.

"Not once did he break away to visit us that entire year—not even for Christmas or Alissa's birthday or our anniversary. All we had were his letters and a false hope that he would one day return.

"He insisted that he had to let his family believe he chose them until he could convince them otherwise that we belonged there. He became consumed with their approval, not grasping that he would never truly get it—not even sacrificing us would do the trick.

"After a little over a year, his father died, and Leigh finally came home to us. But it was not the reunion I yearned for. He regretfully informed me that things did not work out the way he had hoped they would.

"His uncle—now the patriarch of the family—was pleased that Leigh chose to return and demanded that he cut all ties with me forever in order to reclaim his inheritance and place as head of the family business while he retired.

"He had never told them about Alissa. He was waiting for the perfect time, so he said—but before he could, they reinstated him with the threat that if it were to ever come out that he had a child with me, he would lose it all again—and forever this time. So, he kept quiet and led them to believe we were childless."

She stopped to take a breath, the sword stabbing through her heart once again and tears fighting to come to the surface like high tide approaching. Looking over at our mother, pale and saddened, she was that lost little girl reliving her abandonment and shame for being born. I was already beginning to understand why we were never told about this man.

"How naïve Leigh was. They had to have known about Alissa when they threatened him. If they were able to find us, then they'd know we had a child. That stipulation was a test to see if he was worthy of his fortune and where his loyalties were. It still sickens me to think about that family and the lengths they would take to get what they wanted.

"But Leigh said he did it all to protect us. His family was powerful after all—no telling what they would do in the name of preventing a scandal, he warned.

"He swore he would find a loophole though, because he couldn't live without us. He proclaimed that once his uncle died, the reigns would be completely his and he could reunite with us—no one would be able to take what was 'ours' away from us again.

"Even though I begged him one last time to reconsider, reminding him that the money wasn't important to us, he kissed us both goodbye for what would be the last time and set off in his delusional pursuit of a happily ever after.

"I knew better than to wait for that man. He had made his decision and I was going to make mine. I knew that he would lose everything if I demanded he come back or if they 'found out' about Alissa. I had every right to be spiteful and destroy him. I was tempted to show up on their doorstep with our beautiful child and leave him no choice but to acknowledge us. But I didn't.

"He left us alone. He broke his promises and crushed our hearts; yet, I could not bring myself to betray the love of my life, even though he had abandoned us. All I could do was pick up the pieces and move on.

"I appealed to him in a letter for a divorce—something that was not easy to do in our time. By the grace of God and the power of his family's money, our marriage was dissolved. Like it had never even existed. Without an attempt to reconcile or a plea for me to just wait for him a little longer.

"He just let it happen. He didn't fight for us like I had

prayed for.

"Only few months later, I saw the news about his widely publicized nuptials to the original woman he was betrothed to—a woman named Julia Perkins. Yes, this lawyer's great aunt," she added in acknowledgment to the connection.

Now it made sense why she was so thrown off guard by him. I'd save that line of questioning for another time—there was more to that particular story, too, I bet.

"I knew all I needed to know in that moment and declared that this part of my life was over forever. I was never going to look back, and neither was my daughter. Breaking my heart was one thing. But how he could leave behind his little diamond—that's what he called your mom—I will never understand."

The heaviness in the room was all-consuming; the grief of a mother and daughter remembering the moment their life changed forever, bringing forth the memory of a man they swore to forget. My heart went out to them. No family should ever have to bear that kind of pain.

But her story had not ended there. With a few more deep breaths and a delicate tissue to her watery eyes, Granny found the strength to continue.

"It was so difficult to move on. In the back of my mind, I fantasized that this was just a nightmare and that my Leigh would come running back to my arms. That he would disown his family once again to choose our love, to choose our own beautiful family that we created together.

"But reality hit hard and I knew he was never coming back ever again.

"Now an unwed single mother, I was the outcast of the community. Its own Hester Prynne, shame and all. I didn't know what to do.

"My mother became sick only a few weeks later and I was faced with taking care of her at the same time. I had to sell her home and move her in to live with us, which helped to pay for some of her medical care and our day-to-day living expenses, thankfully.

"Her doctor would make house calls to check on us, and he eventually grew a soft spot in his heart for our little family. He'd stop by with extra food from the market or a warm blanket for the cold nights. He never judged us or our situation.

"Consumed by his profession, he didn't have the time to properly court a woman, but his heart was pure gold and he wanted a family to love. He was kind and genuine. He had a great sense of humor and could make me laugh even in my saddest times. He was no Leigh, but that was a good thing, I decided.

"I knew I could never let my heart love like that again. It was dangerous and careless and only caused grief. But I could accept the love of a good man. One who was there by my side as my mother passed away and who loved me and most importantly, my daughter, as his own. It was then that I decided to marry my Harry—your Pops—and we became the Mahoneys.

"Our community knew our story and I wanted to distance myself from the past, so we left town for a fresh start. When we came upon sweet little Armonk, we agreed it was the perfect place to begin our new life together.

"Alissa was almost eight by then and old enough to understand that although Harry was not her biological father, that he was her dad in every other sense of the word. So, to rest of the world, he became her 'real' father and no one was ever the wiser.

"He was so good to us. He loved us until his dying

day—and he loved you girls as his own as well. Turns out, he was unable to have children himself, as we tried with no success, so he was grateful for the child he had in Alissa; we were all the family he ever wanted.

"When Alissa was a little older, I explained the truth in detail about Leigh and she agreed to live out the story that Harry was her father and to never reveal the identity or story of her true lineage. Sadly for her, Leigh never tried to reach out to us again. I read in the papers about twenty years ago how his uncle had died, and still nothing.

"Here he was, finally the patriarch, and still too spineless to try to find out where we were and reunite with his daughter. Never to learn about her life or any grandchildren he may have had.

"I suppose that's why I am so rattled that this young man showed up with such news today. It brings up so many questions of my own.

"How is it that he knew all of your names and where to find us—and so quickly after Leigh's death? How does he have a fortune to leave behind when he clearly violated the 'no heirs' stipulation? It both concerns me and angers me on a whole new level."

A glazed look came across her eyes as she stared off into the distance. A painful acceptance of a truth that hurt harder than the lie she told herself all these years.

"Leigh knew exactly where we were all along, all this time, but he never came back." Now she let the tears fall freely as her face fell into her hands and she began to sob with the deepest of heartbreaks. "He never came back."

3

We didn't know what to say after that. We already learned so much, and witnessed too many raw emotions, to probe any further. The agony of remembering weakened Granny physically, and with a daughter's care, our mother lifted her from the couch to grab her coat and cane.

"Mama, let's get you home."

She shot us a despondent look, mixed with desperation and a seeking of empathy, and we knew we had to put this on hold. Besides, this was a lot to absorb and we all needed time to review chapter one. Who knew how many more there were in this secret prequel?

With big, soft hugs and a bunch of genuine "I love yous," we sent them on their way. The three of us settled back down onto the couch to sort through the debris of an ancestry bomb.

"Wow." Mia was the one to break the silence this time.

"You can say that again," Marissa muttered.

A few moments passed. I'm not sure any of us could formulate a comment or question or starting point. What we had just been told changed everything we had known about our life. We had this mystery grandfather who abandoned Mom and Granny, and yet here he is risen from the dead with an enigmatic will.

"So, what do you think the old geezer wants with us

now?" Marissa's delivery not only broke the silence but gave us the much-needed breath of laughter.

"Maybe his family has disowned him after all and he needs someone to pay for his casket," I quipped, defaulting to my typical sarcasm whenever situations became intense. Awkward vulnerability was never a strong point of mine.

"Or maybe he left us a shitload of money!" Marissa hooted.

"Or maybe there is more to the story and we're about to find out." Mia's somber perspective brought us back to the reality of the situation.

"I guess there is only one way to find out," I offered, fingering the business card left behind by the alluring Joshua Perkins.

"I'll call and set the appointment if you want," offered Marissa, trying to casually steal the sexy lawyer's coveted card from my grasp. I'm pretty sure neither of us cared that he was related through some long lost connection—not like he'd be blood and taboo.

"Set the appointment—or a date? I didn't notice a wedding ring," teased Mia, who could sense the potential sister fight brewing like pungent morning coffee.

"I didn't think he'd be your type, Mar. He wore a suit, seemed to have a respectable job—you sure you want to get mixed up with that kind of hoodlum?"

"Oh, shut up," she laughed as she threw a sage green couch pillow at my head.

"Well, whoever calls him, we should do this right away. I know it must be a lot for Granny and Mom, but I have so many questions still. I don't want to wait to find out what our Grandfather Marino wants.

"I have a feeling there is more to this surprise will

reading than a simple secret spoiler or inheritance announcement. Something bigger is going on. I just know it." As the wife of a cop, Mia's secondhand training had her instincts alert—and she was usually never far off.

"I agree. I can call the office now and have all my meetings canceled for tomorrow and just stay here the night—if that's all right with you, Mi."

"Of course!"

"And I don't have a shift until four tomorrow, so maybe we can get this Mr. Perkins to schedule the reading for the morning and I'll crash here, too," Marissa offered in agreement. "I'm assuming he is not from this town, so he most likely would be available and willing to resolve the matter before heading back home. I'll just give Jay a call to let him know I won't be home."

Jay, as she just enlightened us, was Marissa's newest roommate since Tony moved out; an old friend she alleges to never have slept with. We hoped for her sake, she'd keep it that way instead of playing hot potato with her new apartment pal. As her best friend of almost thirty years, we actually liked the guy and thought he was a good influence in her life.

"Okay, I'll call Mr. Perkins right now and see if I can make it happen—since I'm the only one who won't try to get a date out of it," Mia ribbed as she picked up her cell to dial the number.

The room was fraught with anxiety like a medical intern about to cut open his very first patient. No one was able to sleep a wink from either rehashing the discovery of a lost grandfather or from facing ghosts of the past.

But we were all together again—this time at Mom and

Granny's. Since the emotional turmoil had the biggest effect on Granny, we thought it best to do this from the comfort of her own home.

In a place much smaller than Mia's, though just as endearing, we sat awaiting more information about Leigh Marino.

Mom moved in with Granny right after our dad died, believing that downsizing to the smaller little white ranch home would be better for both of them. The one level structure was ideal, without stairs or excess rooms to fuss about.

It was always inviting—exactly what a grandmother's home should feel like. Apple-scented lit candles, crocheted blankets on the couches and treats waiting on the counter for us, even though we were grown adults. In an instant, you could be whisked back to more youthful times.

The living room boasted a deep off-white carpet that your feet sunk into like quicksand and beautiful rose-patterned throws over the super comfortable green recliner couches. It was here that we chose to gather, rather than at a stiff kitchen table.

"Thank you for making yourself available to meet with us on such short notice, Mr. Perkins," began my mother.

"Of course. I wish our meeting could have been under different circumstances," he said as he stole a glance at Marissa, who was shamelessly wearing a tight knit leopard dress and high heeled black boots, with her long hair slicked back into a high sleek fashion ponytail.

How is it that she just so happened to have that outfit stashed in an overnight bag in her car? Maybe I shouldn't ask.

"Again, my deepest condolences to you all," he uttered

with genuine sincerity, dressed sharply and expensively in black pinstripe this time, I noted to myself.

"We didn't even know the man." Closing my eyes to pray for patience, I placed a gentle hand on Marissa's arm followed by a look of *that's enough*. And she wondered why we all mothered her?

"Yes, right. Well, as I mentioned last night, we are here today as per the wishes of Mr. Leigh Marino for the reading of his will. His instructions on how this was to be carried out were very clear, if not peculiar."

"Peculiar? How so, Mr. Perkins?" probed my mother.

"Well, Mrs. Rossi, you see—Mr. Marino requested two different will readings. One for the Marino family and a separate one for the Rossi family. He thought that given the history of the family dynamics, that it would be uncomfortable to bring everyone under one roof."

"I see. How considerate of him. Or perhaps Mr. Marino is a coward even in death and cannot bring himself to tell his real family about his shameful one." Granny's words cut through the atmosphere like a butcher knife.

"Actually Mrs. Mahoney, the Marino family is aware of your existence. I cannot give you any details beyond that, but they are aware."

"Fine. Carry on," she spat as she muttered what I could have sworn were a whole bunch of Irish curse words. I didn't even know she knew Irish. Then again, as I was coming to find out, I didn't know as much about her as I thought I did.

"In addition to wanting to keep the families separate—for whatever his reason," he paused to acknowledge, "he also had additional letters and documents drawn up. There is his official will, which was read the evening of his burial to the Marino family. And it was requested to be read again once we located your family.

"After the official will is read, I am then instructed to open and deliver the contents of this sealed envelope, addressed solely to the Rossi family."

"And *you* are the chosen one to read it to us, Mr. Perkins?" Granny asked curiously, as she emphasized his name in connection to the woman who married her Leigh.

"Yes, ma'am. I am his lawyer of record," he replied a bit defensively. "I am here—unbiased—on his behalf. However, you should know, I am only to deliver the sealed letters. I am not privy to their contents."

I could have sworn I saw him shift a little in his seat and loosen yet another expensive Gucci tie. I'm not quite sure this man was prepared for such a tough crowd—we were more intimidating than a courtroom full of witch hunt justice seekers in a murder case. But for a prominent lawyer (you bet I looked him up), he certainly was a nervous nelly behind all the hyped up glam.

"Your ex-husband was not very forthcoming about the contents of this envelope and, even as his lawyer, I have not been permitted to see them. After I read the official will to all of his heirs, as all of them must be named in the will whether they receive anything or not, I am instructed to leave this envelope—the one and only copy—with you, never to be read by the Marino family.

"Whatever this envelope contains is meant for your family and your family alone."

"Okay, then let's get to it," said Marissa as she kicked up her feet into a reclined position and folded her arms back behind her head as if ready to sun herself.

"Great. Please bear with me as I am required to read through the document in its entirety. This is going to take a while."

"I'll put up some tea," Granny offered.

"I'll grab the shot glasses and whiskey," Marissa countered.

With everyone settled with their choice of tea or whiskey (or both), we were all ready to hear what Grandfather Leigh had to say to us all. If nothing else, perhaps this would bring some clarity and closure. It still felt surreal—was this a bona fide family mystery like I read about in my many young adult novels?

"Everyone ready?" After a room full of nods, he began. So serious, so professional. *So dang hot.*

I, Leigh Marino, resident in the City of Cobble Hill, County of Brooklyn, State of New York, being of sound mind, not acting under duress or undue influence, and fully understanding the nature and extent of all my property and of this disposition thereof, do hereby make, publish, and declare this document to be my Last Will and Testament, and hereby revoke any and all other wills and codicils heretofore made by me.

He then read a series of legal mumbo jumbo about expenses and taxes and the appointment of himself as personal representative before getting to the "disposition of property" portion of the will. I could have fallen asleep listening to the man drone on about the different properties, art galleries, restaurants and other nonsense given to these strangers—sorry, *family members.*

However, I was absolutely captivated by how damn rich this man must have been…and annoyed over the amount of crap he left his adopted son and family. He really left my mother behind for all of this?

It then came time for our acknowledgments.

To my ex-wife, Lillith Mahoney and daughter, Alissa Rossi: Deed to Home in Charlton, New York. Also to Lillith, our gold wedding band.

We all took a deep breath as he paused and handed my grandmother a small, solid, worn-out gold band and two white, sealed envelopes addressed in old school calligraphy.

"A deed to a home?" Mia asked incredulously.

"In Charlton?" Granny could barely choke back the impending sobs as her weak fingers slid along the top of the one envelope to reveal an official deed with her and Mom's names on it.

"Yes, Mrs. Mahoney. It is my understanding that Mr. Marino had purchased and restored the original home you and your daughter grew up in. He also made arrangements for taxes to be paid for the duration of your ownership."

Wonder filled her and my mother's eyes. Bittersweet at least. A home mixed with the emotions of true love and happiness, then abandonment and betrayal. How is it that he never bothered with them, but then planned to restore and bequeath them an entire house? It's absurd.

She held on to the second envelope, sensing the privacy of its contents, already over-processing why she was left a memory-ridden old dwelling.

"May I continue?" he asked gently.

We collectively consented, wondering what the next grenades to drop would be.

To my daughter, Alissa Rossi: My mother's pearl necklace, earrings and ring set.

A plastic bag containing stunning, delicate pearls set into what I imagined were expensive cuts of diamonds was handed to her, along with her own letter. She took it carefully, almost in awe of such a valuable trinket.

"I may have been six when I last remember seeing him, but I do recall his stories about his mother. Lena, her name was. He was very fond of her and I always wished I could have met her. She felt special to me for some reason—not like the rest of Marino side," she remembered contemplatively.

Mr. Perkins continued on, growing annoyed at our interrupting commentary. Like we weren't permitted to handle this awkward situation in our own way? *Keep it shut, Meg,* I scolded myself.

To my granddaughters, Megan Rossi, Mia Logan and Marissa Rossi: plane tickets to Shannon, Ireland; Florence, Italy; and Barcelona, Spain, all three trips of which must be taken within a year of my death.

A single letter with our names on it was handed to Mia, who was sitting closest.

"Wow. That's an unusual inheritance to receive. I wonder what that is all about?" I inquired.

"I am pretty sure the letters will explain in more detail, but it is my understanding that each of these trips holds tokens for you that are in the possession of distant relatives in Ireland, Italy and Spain. They are from his mother's side, the O'Sullivans."

"The O'Sullivans?" Even Granny didn't recognize the name.

"Yes. That is his mother's maternal bloodline," he continued. "In order to leave this part of his family anything, Leigh had to work a loophole. There was a stipulation in his uncle's will about the Marino property never going to unknown heirs, should they be revealed."

"You mean to the bastards?" muttered my mother, quite bitterly. It was a side of her that was rarely shown, but we'd call it the "off with her head" Mom voice when we were kids. We knew to run for cover when the Red Queen in her came out.

"Mrs. Rossi, I mean no disrespect. I am only passing along what I learned, as much as I do know. Leigh did share with me that he had many regrets in his life, yet still had to honor his uncle's provisions.

"Even though it came to light somehow that he did in fact have an heir with Lillith, the Marino family collectively decided not to remove Leigh as head of the family. With Rocco deceased and a more modern acceptance of family skeletons, they upheld Leigh's position with the condition that this line would never be eligible for any of the Marino legacy; past, present or future.

"It was all agreed that instead of Marino heirlooms and property, he would be allowed to pass on some family trinkets from his mother's side to you, as they would not be contested by the Marino family or be in violation of his uncle's wishes. Even the home in Charlton was purchased and restored with O'Sullivan family money generously donated by one of his cousins.

"And, as per full disclosure, this was revealed at the Marino family will reading. As the O'Sullivans are part of the maternal heritage and not considered by them as their direct family bloodline, they had no objection and will not protest your receipt of these tokens. So, they are yours, without contest. The paperwork was already signed."

As if trying to make our grandfather's bequeathed gifts mean something, he added quietly, "It was all he was able to do under the circumstances."

"We understand, Mr. Perkins. Thank you," said Mia, trying to smooth over the room full of gym resistance bands ready to snap. "I am sure they are lovely. And we are grateful for such a wonderful travel opportunity."

Looking over at us in her motherly way, she cautioned, "We will have to talk about it first."

I gave her the respect of a nod, while Marissa rolled her eyes—*hmm,* I wonder where our nieces and nephew get it from.

"If you'll permit me, I am required to read the remainder of his will to completion."

Joshua Perkins proceeded to go through more legalese concerning omission, bond, the very specific discretionary powers bestowed upon him as Leigh's personal representative (which I still questioned myself), "contesting beneficiary" and so on and so forth. He ended by folding the will back up into an envelope and handing it to my grandmother to keep.

"So, question for you." Why did I raise my hand up like a school girl?

"Yes, Megan."

"When reading about the other family members, I couldn't help but notice that his stepson and step-grandchildren carry the name of Marino. Why's that?"

"Well, when he married Julia, he accepted her son David as his own. Since David's father was deceased, Leigh thought for the sake of family it would be best to legally adopt him and give him the Marino name, as he would be the only one able to carry on his legacy.

"Unfortunately, Julia and Leigh were unable to conceive a child of their own together, so the name continues to pass on through David's heirs."

"So, just like Mom became a Mahoney, David became a Marino," Mia connected.

"Exactly," he agreed.

"Interesting how some other woman's child is acceptable as an heir, but not my mother," spouted Marissa.

"It's just the way of the rich," bit back Granny. "Money forgives transgressions of money. Not to mention, having a male child is more favorable as an heir than a daughter to them. Such cavemen."

Mom looked distraught by that comment—by the whole morning.

"Oh, Alissa, I am so sorry. I should be more sensitive. I didn't mean to upset you," regretted Granny.

"Mama, you have nothing to apologize for. It's reality. It wouldn't do any of us good to pretend otherwise. I have a happy life, filled with a wonderful mother and three beautiful daughters, a kind son-in-law I love like a son and amazing grandchildren. There is nothing some estranged father could ever give me that would be worth more than what I already have."

We all came together to form a big group hug. Smiles broke out, almost forgetting that our grandfather's lawyer was even still in the room.

"I'm sorry, there is just one more piece of business to tend to. I have some paperwork for all of you to sign, acknowledging the reading, receipt of items, relinquishing your right to further contest the distribution of property and so forth. That is, unless you do have an objection?"

"I do," defied Marissa. "I'm the artist of the family. What if I want a piece of that art gallery he passed down to some distant second cousin once removed or something of mine? Aren't I entitled to fight that?"

"Marissa!" We were all dismayed by her outburst—though why should we be? It's Marissa, after all. The kind of woman who always wanted to know why she was down on the bottom of the seesaw when others were at the top, not seeing the big picture that life is a movement of balance.

"Oh, relax. It's hypothetical." She turned to the nervous lawyer with her challenging fire. "What if I did want to protest?"

He let out a stifled laugh. "Forgive me. That felt like déjà vu. You reminded me of Leigh's granddaughter-in-law, Peggy, just now. She's married to his grandson Patrick and had the same kind of question about if they wanted a part in the O'Sullivan inheritances. She wasn't serious of course—just curious, even if characteristically materialistic by nature.

"But to answer your question, you would need to go through a whole bunch of legal channels and court hearings to fight it. In the end though, Ms. Rossi, I must tell you that due to Rocco Marino's prior will conditions, most likely you would be denied because you are a descendant of Mrs. Mahoney.

"The living Marinos have already bent the rules as it is. It doesn't make it right—it's just how it is. It's always possible to win, but unlikely."

"Of course, Mr. Perkins," said Granny as she looked him directly in the eye. "We will all"—now looking directly at Marissa—"be happy to sign whatever documents you need us to, so you can be on your way. We will not be contesting anything. We thank you for your time."

With a few quick signatures and a short goodbye, the relieved messenger boy was on his way.

While mild chatter broke out among everyone, I took the opportunity to question Granny about him in private.

"Granny, I couldn't help but notice that it bothered you that Mr. Perkins is our grandfather's lawyer."

"Ah, my clever girl. You don't miss anything. It's nothing to do with him personally," she took my hand in hers and smiled broadly. No one else ever looked at me with that kind of pride for having a brain like my Granny did—except maybe Daddy.

"I was just taken by surprise, that's all—though I shouldn't be. Generational social circles and loyalties are still common these days in rich families. Leigh would want someone he already knew and trusted as his lawyer and advisor.

"What I am surprised about is how *gracious*," she winced sarcastically, "the Marinos were in letting us have anything at all. My Leigh was a smart one, though. I'm interested to see what kind of loophole he was able to get past his family, that's for certain."

With that, I turned to the rest of the room on cue. "I think it's time to see what these curiously classified letters have in store for us."

Everyone agreed that we would open our letters and read them to each other.

Although we were concerned that Granny and Mom might have more private messages they should keep to themselves, they declared that there had been enough secrecy, and that it was time to bring it all out into the open.

Ripping the bandaid off her scar, Granny went first.

My dearest Lillith,

I have no right to even call you dearest, but it is how I still feel about you after all these years. I can only imagine the shock this must bring to you. I have no desire to hurt you or open old wounds. I thought the only way you would listen to me after all these years would be through death. I only hope this letter reaches you in time.

I have thought of you and our sweet Alissa every day since the moment I left you both behind in our beautiful home. The looks on your faces burned into my mind that day and have haunted me my entire life.

I am not a real man. A real man would have denied these material demands, this pathetic attempt for approval, and chosen love. For that, I will never forgive myself.

Although this will serve as no consolation to you, I lived a very unhappy, dutiful life. Marrying Julia meant nothing—I had no love left in my heart for anyone after you requested our divorce. I vowed to never love again because I did not deserve it. Just as I did not deserve you.

I wanted to fight for us; to deny the divorce. But my hands were tied, and I was weak. There was nothing I could do but have mercy and let you go, hoping that you would live a wonderful life without me.

Many times, I wanted to risk it all to return to see our beautiful Alissa grow up; to have more babies with you like we planned and travel the world together.

I confess, I did make secret trips to check in on you both. I saw the sadness and struggle and I couldn't bear to make it worse by revealing myself. I was ashamed of my weakness, knowing I had caused all of this pain. But as time went on, I saw your happiness return. Happiness in the form of Arthur Mahoney.

I was genuinely pleased for you, my Lillith. You found a good man for yourself and our baby girl. He was ten times the man I could ever be and so I told myself it was a blessing that I had left.

After that, I kept tabs but returned sparingly as it was too agonizing to watch. The family began to wonder about my frequent trips and since I had chosen duty to them, I had responsibilities to uphold. And you to protect. I feared for what they might do to you. A coward's life, indeed.

As I near death and reflect on life, I can say for certain that leaving you and Alissa behind was my one regret. None of the money in the world or the phony acceptance of my family ever matched the depth of love and worthiness that I experienced with you.

I leave you my gold wedding band not as a mere token or a painful reminder; but as proof that my love for you never died. I looked at it every night to remember how good life once was.

You will remain forever my one true love; and in my final words, I extend my sincerest apologies for not being the man you loved, needed or deserved. I deserted you, and for that, I would never ask for your forgiveness.

Just know that for my entire life, I mourned all that I had given up and I suffered the consequences. Maybe knowing that will bring you some solace.

May what I am about to set in motion be my final act of contrition as I attempt to rectify all that I have taken from my one true family.

Farewell mo shíorghrá,
Leigh

We all sat in silence for a while, allowing Granny her moment to grieve what obviously was a deep love. Her blue eyes were more gray today, like a cloudy sky awaiting the jolt of a thunderstorm. Her hair a lighter white, a few more wrinkles around her pink-lipsticked mouth. This whole experience was aging her and her heart. After a few minutes, she finally spoke.

"I always wondered if he regretted leaving us. Now I know. For the record, I don't take any joy from his agony," she sighed, ever the compassionate human being.

"He was right about one thing though—he was not the man I deserved. But he *was* the man I loved." Tears fell gently from her glassy eyes like the beginning trickle of a new waterfall.

"Oh, Granny," I whispered as I hugged her to me. "I'm so sorry."

"Granny? What does '*mo shiorghrá*' mean?" Mia queried softly.

"Ah. It's Gaelic for 'My Eternal Love.' It is how he always signed his letters to me—even his final letter granting a divorce. I don't doubt that I was his great love. I just wish we were enough for him."

"Mama, we *were* enough. I never knew he came back to check on us."

"Neither did I."

"I still have so many unanswered questions."

"Mom, why don't you open your letter? Maybe it will answer them," I offered.

"Okay." With trembling, well-manicured hands, my mother daintily opened her envelope with a letter opener, as if wanting to preserve every last piece of what he left her.

My Little Diamond,

My, how you have grown into such a beautiful woman, just like your mother. I know you may find this hard to believe, but I have watched you grow from that spunky little girl to an even classier, bolder woman.

I admit today that I have been there through most of your milestones. From a distance, but I was there.

I was hidden in the back rows of both your high school and college graduations. I was in a car parked down the street as you posed for pictures wearing that gorgeous teal blue dress that highlighted your eyes for the prom. I had half a mind to follow you and your date to make sure he remained a gentleman, but I had a feeling you could handle yourself.

I blended into the pews at the church on your wedding day and never felt so breathless in my life as when I saw you walk down that aisle in your mother's dress (oh yes, I noticed).

I wished more than anything to give you your grandmother's pearls that day and bless your union as I handed you over to the very worthy Joseph Rossi. You chose well, my darling daughter.

When I received notification of the birth of each of your beautiful daughters, I made arrangements to pass by the nursery window off hours so I could glance at the treasures I would never get to hold.

I stood in disguise among the mourners of your dear father, Arthur, wanting to reach out and comfort you. I have been among the crowds who came in droves to hear your literary speeches. You have the brilliance and beauty of your mother—and thankfully, her courage. Your stubbornness, however, seems to come from me.

I never revealed myself because I did not believe it was my place to be intrusive; plus, I was too much of a coward to jeopardize my family arrangement. I only wanted to be a part of your life, in whatever way I could be, yet honor my agreement with your mother and my uncle. But I just couldn't live without watching my precious diamond grow up.

I know you will come to hear about my stepson, who I adopted and gave my last name to. Out of no disrespect to the fine young man that I helped to raise, giving him my name was not the same as giving you life.

You must know, my daughter, that no child on this earth ever replaced you. You still remain, to this day, my one and only baby.

The child born out of the only love I ever had to give; the best piece of me will live on in you.

I never once forgot about you, sweetheart. I loved you with all my heart and soul and became a broken man when I left you. Know that you never did anything wrong. You did not deserve a father's abandonment.

But also know that even though I never reclaimed you, I never truly left. Though I am not sure that will bring you any comfort for what I have done.

I am so proud of you. You are beautiful, smart, kind, graceful—everything a father could ever wish for in a daughter. You have undoubtedly passed those traits on to your own daughters—courtesy also of a very good man. Had things been different in life, I would have been proud to have called him my son. I am so sorry you lost him so young.

I cannot take away your pain. I cannot give you back the years together I stole from you. I cannot make up for lost time or apologize enough for not being a good father.

All I can do is leave you with the only promise I never broke: I loved you every second, of every minute, of every day since the moment you came into this world. And the truth is, your sparkle never left my heart.

With all the love I have,
Your Father, Leigh

Mom carefully folded back the letter and delicately placed it back into the envelope as if it could shatter like glass if mishandled. We allowed her time to digest what she had learned.

"That was…intense." Marissa spoke for us all after a few moments had passed.

"Mom, how do you feel about all of this?"

She looked over at Mia sullenly in response. There was no shortage of crying today, as these letters were gut-wrenching. Mom straightened up in her chair to gather her thoughts before she spoke.

"It's a lot to take in, actually. The fact that he watched me grow up and was really at all those milestones, but never approached me, is quite a shock."

"Kinda creepy though, isn't it?" I couldn't help but nudge Marissa after her ill-timed insensitivity. Really? No filter at all?

"I can see how it would seem creepy to you girls," she managed with an amused smile, used to Marissa's antics. "But to me, it's not. It's actually endearing—and also angering. How I wished he would be there for all those special occasions in my life and then to find out he really was, but never let me know? It's going to take a while to sort it out."

"Of course, it will," Mia pulled Mom's hands into hers and stroked them. "A whole lifetime of beliefs has just been uprooted. It is going to take time for you—for Granny, for all of us—to come to terms with everything we have learned over the last few days."

Sensing the emotion of the room, I decided we needed to take a break.

"You know what? Why don't we talk a walk down to the water? I think we could all use some fresh air—and I do love those cranberry-orange scones from Julio's Bakery. Come on, it will be good for us."

My sisters immediately perked up at the idea, but Mom and Granny were hesitant.

"You know what, dears?" started Granny. "Why don't you go on without us? I think your mother and I could use a few minutes alone to work through our feelings and grief. How about you bring us back some scones and we'll put up some tea?"

I smiled big at her, understanding perfectly. "You betcha, Granny. I'll even pick up a few of those chocolate raspberry petit fours you like, just for you."

Our walk down to the water was eerily quiet. The waves were practically still as we approached the worn, wooden dock that surrounded it. We found some equally tattered benches to sit on, feeling the warmth of the sun and the slightest of breezes blowing through our hair.

A hint of spring teased us, as we patiently waited for the winter cold to subside. The only sounds were that of a few delicate wave crashes and some pesky seagulls chirping for food. A solemn moment, indeed.

"So, that was something," said Marissa, breaking the silence.

"I can't even imagine what Mom and Granny are going through right now," Mia said with her usual empathy. "I mean, to first live with the pain of the abandonment, then to live with a suppressed lie, for it all to come out unexpectedly and change everything they ever thought to be true. I'm heartbroken for them."

"Me too." I let a beat skip before revealing what had been swimming like salmon upstream in my head for the last hour. "Hey, did you guys pick up on what he said at the end of Granny's letter?"

"The Gaelic thing?" Marissa wondered.

"No. The part that said something about 'may what

I am about to set in motion be my final act of contrition'
stuff. Don't you think that was cryptic?"

"Yeah, that *was* kind of puzzling. What do you think
it means?"

"Maybe he just meant how he acknowledged us in the
will or brought our presence to light after being hidden all
these years," Mia offered.

"No, I don't think that's it. I think there is more to
this story. Something is tugging at me. I feel like our little
trips have something to do with it. Call it a hunch."

"Well, speaking of the trips," began Mia. "I don't
know how feasible it is for the three of us to take all of
these trips. Especially within the course of a year."

"Mi, you are getting ahead of yourself," I cut her off,
not wanting to endure her maternal perspective on why
this may or may not be a good idea. "We don't even know
the details of this just yet. Maybe it is one trip per person.
Or maybe they are weekend jaunts or one after the other
over a simple week or two. Let's just wait and see what
our letter has to say." I was anxious to read it, but I knew
the others needed some space and time to absorb the new
information.

Still, I couldn't help but feel my heart soar with
excitement in between the chaos. Ireland? Italy? Spain?
It's like a dream to me to be able to explore all these
wonderful places; I already had my bags packed in my
head.

Although I have been to a number of foreign
countries through my corporate travels, including Italy,
it was always quick and too business-like to be able to
truly enjoy the cultures. Sightseeing was never on those
agendas. Though I did know London inside and out like
a second home.

My workaholic personality prevented me from truly living in the moment or unearthing all that the journeys had to offer like my father so often did. This was a once-in-a-lifetime opportunity to make some bucket list wishes come true and I was going with or without the agreement of my sisters. Though, I was pretty sure that Marissa also had stars in her eyes.

"Well, I for one am intrigued by it all," she said as if reading my mind. "Do you think we gave them enough time? Maybe we should have brought the envelope with us."

"No, that wouldn't be right. We promised to read our letters in front of each other. After hearing and seeing how vulnerable Granny and Mom were with theirs, we owe it to them to stay in this together."

"Mia's right. Though it is getting a bit chilly. I think it's okay for us to start heading back. But—bakery first!"

With decadent pastries in hand, we walked back to our beautiful family home. We shared so many wonderful memories here. Granny still had the old-fashioned tire swing on the tree, where we would twirl each other until we were dizzy.

Then there was the worn-out mini-house in the backyard that Daddy built with his bare hands for whenever we visited our grandparents—a tree house was too dangerous, he told us, so he made one on the ground.

We even bought a mini toy kitchen set to go inside. Oh, how we loved to play in there for hours. I'd clean, Mia would cook and Marissa would pretend to decorate. Now all tattered and weathered, full of cobwebs, dirt and insects, it still had a magical charm to it. My, had life been so much simpler then.

We arrived to find Mom busy in the kitchen gathering everything for tea, while Granny was sitting at the dining room table simply looking out into the distance through the large bay window. It was melancholy inside their usually energetic house. Faces worn from weeps, eyes weakened from emotion, it was clear that this whole situation was weighing heavily on them.

Even though I was dying inside to read our letter, I didn't want to be selfish. It had been a hard day already and who knows what other surprises were waiting to pop out like a jack-in-the-box.

"You know, why don't we just read this another time? We've had enough for one day."

"Nonsense," said Granny, though the words came out as barely a whisper. "Just because I am a bit sad doesn't mean that we have to call it quits. Now, just sit yourselves down. Let's have some tea and scones while we have a listen to what good old Leigh had to say to three granddaughters he never met."

On cue, Mom entered the room with her crème-colored Lenox teapot with matching sugar bowl, creamer, teacups and saucers. She was always so stylish when serving—even when it was just us sitting around casually like this. She brought in an assortment of herbal teas, knowing our tastes were as unique as our personalities.

Mia followed suit, presenting our scones daintily on yet another matching Lenox tray, accompanied by whipped butter and some orange marmalade Granny always kept on hand from a local farmers market. I added the rich petit fours as promised to the platter.

After settling down with our teas and desserts, the awkward silence ensued.

"Let's see what our mystery is all about, shall we?" Marissa nudged Mia.

"Meg, as the oldest, why don't you go ahead and read the letter to all of us?" Mom suggested.

Obliging, I took the letter from a willing Mia and carefully opened it, inhaling sharply. I somehow knew that whatever I was about to read would change our future. Maybe not in this exact moment—but our lives were never going to be the same.

My Darling Granddaughters, Megan, Mia & Marissa,

I know all of this might have come as quite a shock to you, hearing about some old grandfather who abandoned your mother and grandmother. Why would you care about my death when you never knew me in life?

I would not blame you for your anger or confusion, but I ask that you allow a dying man a final wish to help set things right.

I loved your grandmother and mother with all of my heart— so much so, that I left them because I believed they would be better without me. I lived in great sorrow day after day, regretting my decision.

But that is neither here nor there. I cannot change the past or your impression of me. I have watched you grow into strong, beautiful women and I know your loyalty runs deep. You all remind me of different parts of my own grandmother, Alessia— my mother's mother—and it is through her spirit of love and family that I write to you today.

In my will, I bequeathed you three trips to be taken within a year of my death. These trips are more than just for your travel pleasure, though I do hope that they bring you great joy. They are about reclaiming your own lost heritage, one that is not associated with the patriarchal Marino clan, but that of your ancestral O'Sullivan line.

I knew that there would be no objection to the will for trips or tokens left to you three because they are from O'Sullivan blood. But what is unknown to the Marinos is the depth of treasure that the O'Sullivans (and extended family branches) hold.

It was a sacred secret held onto through the generations as a result of family shame—one that could only be passed down to those worthy of knowing without judgment or betrayal.

My mother withheld it from my father; he never knew her family's true legacy, nor did he care. He was too absorbed in protecting his Marino name. On her deathbed, not too long after my father's own passing, she called to me and revealed the truth of her lineages.

Now as I am on mine, I will pass on the legacy and history to you. But first you must make these journeys to meet with your rightful kin. Awaiting you in each country is a sacred family heirloom that has been in the possession of my maternal relatives, kept safe for the moment I was ready to bequeath them to you.

All three of you must journey together to each place and learn your heritage as a family. You will find that the gifts you receive will suit each of you quite well.

You will first go to County Mayo, Ireland where you will be welcomed into the home of Colleen O'Sullivan. Colleen is my first cousin and the last of the O'Sullivans, aside from you all. In her possession is an ancient Celtic ring that belonged to my great-grandmother, Elena, though it traces back much further than her generation. This ring shall be passed down to our aptly Celtic-named heir, Megan.

You will then travel to Florence, Italy where my mother's cousin, Sister Maria Bianchi, awaits you. As she is nearing 100 years of age, should she predecease me or your arrival, her lawyer, Francesco Marchesi, will greet you. There awaits a special Italian carved wooden jewelry box to be given to sweet Mia.

Finally, your journey will conclude in Barcelona, Spain. There my distant cousin, Edward John Rubio, will bring the final relic: a rare statue imagined to be sculpted by Francesco de Goya, which shall be presented to the fiery Marissa.

Insert squeal of delight from Marissa while I shot her a quick glare of warning to let me finish.

In order to claim your inheritance, you must follow what I have asked of you. All three together to all three locations within the year. My overseas relatives each have further instructions and information on pre-paid arrangements for your accommodations, meals, travel and spending money during your time away from home. You will need for nothing.

This plan was also designed with the utmost secrecy. In order to protect our legacy and yourselves, I ask for your discretion as well until all is revealed. I cannot emphasize the clandestine nature of this request enough.

May these journeys bring you blessings you never dreamed of and may you remember that your lineage extends far beyond the poor judgment of a selfish man; there is a fantastic ancestry to discover and it is my wish that you embrace it—and life— wholeheartedly.

With love and admiration,

Your Grandfather, Leigh

I put the letter down and looked around the soundless room. Everyone was dealing with the information in their own way. Granny sat straight up, her wrinkled lips puckered in a combination of intrigue and annoyance. My mother was faking a smile—I knew she was genuinely happy for us, but her heart was still too shattered by it all.

Marissa was jonesing to get going—I could see the newly wound up grandfather clock gears turning. I was keeping it together like a professional, but my insides wanted to jump out in childish excitement. Mia looked a bit distracted and downhearted, avoiding eye contact with any of us. I decided to break the ice.

"Well, that is even more mysterious sounding than before I read this. If it's just a ring, statue and jewelry box, can't they just ship it to us? It *is* the 21st century."

"Are you kidding me? Why are you looking a gift horse in the mouth? This sounds like a once-in-a-lifetime *dream*," cried Marissa.

"I agree. It's not every day you receive a gift like this." Mom then smiled affectionately, as if captured in a memory. "I feel like your father would be behind you on this. Almost as if he played a part in making it happen for you."

"You're right. It is pretty exciting! I can't wait!" I turned to Granny. "Would it upset you if we fulfilled Grandfather Leigh's wishes? Just say the word and we can leave this behind."

Granny looked over in a bit of a shock. "My sweet girls," she started, as mini pools formed in her sparkling eyes. "I have waited all my life for Leigh Marino to show me the kind of man he could be. If he wants to right his wrongs through you, there is nothing that would make me happier than to see your own dreams come true."

Without skipping a beat, Marissa started with the plans. "I hated my job anyway. I'm going to march on in to Greg tomorrow and tell him where he can shove it! I'm ready to travel the world on this grandpa's dime! And I'm sure Jay wouldn't mind having a bachelor pad for a while, as long as I can still kick in the rent."

I laughed and joined in the fantasy. "I have accrued so much vacation time over the years of non-stop working, I'm pretty sure I might even have months available! For sure, I have enough to get us started on Ireland as soon as you ladies would like."

"How wonderful!" Mom exclaimed. "Oh, it does my heart good to see you girls be able to do something together. Although I grew up without siblings, I know there is no stronger bond than that of sisters."

"Is there anything in there about how you find these tickets or what the next step is?" Marissa asked.

"I didn't see a P.S. or anything." I checked the envelope again. "Wait…something is in here."

I pulled out a travel agent's business card. "Bingo! I'm guessing Ms. Veronica Ashford of Legacy Travels might have the answers we are looking for."

"Do you want me to call her?"

"Nah, Mar, that's okay. I think we can all agree I am the planner of the family. I can work on getting us all organized. You can research the weather and area and let us know what we should pack and sightsee. And Mia, you would be perfect for figuring out some must-dine restaurants. Oh my gosh, this is so incredible!"

I felt like a little girl about to meet Mickey Mouse for the first time. But Mia didn't look like she wanted to go to our inherited Disneyland; she shuffled on the couch quietly, still avoiding eye contact.

"Mia, honey, what's wrong?" gently probed Mom.

The room quelled, giving Mia a chance to collect her thoughts. She cleared her throat a few times, trying to speak but couldn't, and then started crying uncontrollably into our mother's arms. Mom held on to her tightly, stroking her hair in comfort while looking up at us as confused as we were.

"I'm sorry. I'm so sorry," she sobbed.

"Sorry for what, sweetheart?" my mother crooned, trying to help settle our distraught sister. I joined them on the couch, rubbing Mia's back in sympathy.

Once she calmed herself a bit, and accepted some tissues, she was ready to let it out.

"I'm sorry that I am going to ruin everything for everyone."

"Mi, how could you ruin everything? If you don't want to look for restaurants, it's okay, we can wing it."

"No, no, it's not that." She took a deep breath. "I just—I can't go." And with that, more guilt fell from her eyes like an unexpected storm.

"Why can't you go?" Marissa asked in a soothing, tender voice, as she knelt before her sister.

Shifting moods quickly from sad to indignant, Mia snapped. "You're joking, right? Why can't I go? *Why* can't I go?" She paused a moment, inhaling sharply. What were we missing?

"I have children and a husband to think about. I can't just up and leave them. It must be nice to have your single lives where you can do whatever you want, but I actually have a family to consider. So, I'm sorry to let you and your dreams down, but I'm not going."

"Mia, I—" I stopped myself. We didn't think about her position before getting all worked up. She had a valid point. It was too much to ask of her.

"Mia." Granny turned to face her full on. "Our sweet Mia, always putting everyone ahead of herself," she said as she stroked a piece of hair off her rounded, tear-stained face. "Do you really think you are alone in this?"

A little calmer and more composed, she answered, "Yes, actually, I do."

"My dear, when it comes to dreams, there is always a way. Let this be a lesson to you," she advised grandmotherly. "Your mother and I discussed this possibility while you stepped out to go down to the water and we already called Kevin and filled him in. He is on board with whatever you need to do.

"Mom and I will take turns staying at your house in the guest room to make sure the kids are dressed, fed and taken to school and all of their activities."

"We will take great care of them," Mom chimed in. "You can be at ease, knowing that they are in good hands without disrupting Kevin's schedule, either."

Quietly she whispered, "I can't ask you to do that."

"You didn't ask, now did you?" said Granny. "We offered, knowing what it is like to have that family you do everything for. Knowing that you always put yourself last. Well, now that all on the home front will be taken care of, it is up to you whether you decide to do this or not. For yourself."

"Mi, I am so sorry I didn't think about how difficult this would be for you to get away. It was selfish of me," I began. "But you do also deserve this break. You have a beautiful home and family, one that you postponed your own dreams for because they mean the world to you. Forget me and Marissa for a second. Do you want to go on these trips?"

"I—I would really like to. I just—I don't know if I can leave my children, even in good hands. I've never been away from them for more than a day or two."

"They are not little babies anymore, Mia. I think they would be inspired to see their mother do something so cool," Mom prodded.

She pondered that for a moment. Nervously twisting her tendrils between her fingers, you could tell she was torn.

"I have an idea. Why don't we give you some time to think about it? We have a whole year. A few days or so won't make a big difference," I gestured.

"You know what?" she considered. "No. You are all right. I haven't done anything for myself in years and my heart is so intrigued by this. To learn about some history we never knew about, meet some cousins and see the world? This chance doesn't come along—ever. I would be a fool not to go on an adventure with my sisters."

She coyly grinned and Marissa and I tackled her for a big sister hug, laughing all the way.

"Okay, then. I will call the travel agent tomorrow morning and get it all started. Now, who's up for Chinese food delivery?"

"We will now begin boarding for Flight 452 to Shannon, Ireland," announced an overly chipper attendant over the loudspeaker. Didn't she realize the roosters weren't even awake yet?

"That's us! Are you ready, ladies?" Did Mia realize it? How can anyone be so cheerful in the morning? Even my breasts weren't as perky as she was.

"I know I am," said Marissa, as she quickened to reapply her ruby red lipstick before putting her makeup bag back into her huge black Coach purse. You would think she was about to go to a concert instead of on an eight-hour overseas flight.

Did I mention it was *really* early in the morning?

Mia and I, on the other hand, went for a more casual approach with our flight ensembles. Since it was just the beginning of April, it was still chilly out. The arrival of "spring" meant little to the Northeast region—and even less where we were headed. I was so impulsive in booking the flights, I had forgotten to consider we were headed towards the rainy season in Ireland (well, rainier than normal). Too late to change plans now.

As we boarded the plane, we could barely contain our excitement.

"Can you believe how rich dear old Grampy was? First class tickets and all!"

"I know, Mar! We are certainly going to travel in style." Yes, luxury definitely suited me quite well. With my frequent traveling, I was already used to it, so I was relieved not to be relegated to coach seating on our trips. Sorry, not sorry. I become, shall we say, *particular,* when I travel.

Anyway, as soon we settled onto the plane, I was ready for some celebratory champagne. We took our complementary flutes as we sat in oversized recliner seats and relished in our good fortune.

"Ladies, what should we toast to?" asked Mia.

"To an adventure of a lifetime," I said.

"To the mystery of it all!" chimed in Marissa.

But Mia said it best. "To sisterhood."

We all yelled *Sláinte!* and drank down what must have been a very expensive reserve. The bubbles danced on my tongue before they smoothly tingled the back of my throat. A good reserve, indeed.

The flight was long but made wonderfully relaxing by our first-class accommodations. Personal feather pillows, fleece blankets, eye masks and dedicated televisions were only the tip of the iceberg—the food was spectacularly delectable.

We elected to share a cheeseboard for starters, along with a Midleton Mule with Jameson for Marissa, a Guinness for Mia and a Bailey's Mint Martini for myself. We then ordered one of each of the main dishes so we could savor them all: honey and whiskey grilled salmon with rosemary roasted red potatoes; mustard-crusted pork loin with apple-cabbage slaw; and lentil-mushroom shepherd's pie.

Of course, no smorgasbord was complete without the assorted mini scones served with jam, clotted cream and tea. If this is a sample of what's to come over the next two weeks, I should figure on gaining about ten pounds.

When we arrived at the airport's baggage claim, we were greeted by a big "Rossi" sign, held by a stout little woman with curly gray hair that playfully exposed a few subtle traces of fiery strands. She was wearing long brown pants and a colorfully stitched Galway sweater, but nothing was as bright as her beaming smile and elfish green eyes.

"Are you cousin Colleen?"

"That I am! My goodness! Look at ya—you're as beautiful as deities! C'mere and gimme a hug." She wrapped her big, strong arms around the three of us in a joyful embrace. I loved her instantly.

"Is that all you be taking, is it now?" She had a small baggage trolley alongside her and started to put our bags on it as we tried to object.

"Oh, no. We still need to wait for our luggage. This was just our carry-ons," explained Marissa.

"I tasked Marissa here with letting us know what to bring. Big mistake," I laughed, motioning my thumb over to my sister for easy identification. "I'm afraid we were coaxed into bringing something for every season."

"Hey, you never know!" she giggled.

"I'm Megan, by the way. And this is Mia."

"I'll try to keep ya straight. Do any of you have to go to the jacks before we head out? Long journey ahead, don'tcha know."

"The jacks?" Marissa asked in confusion.

"The ladies room," I offered. Turning to Colleen, "I tried to brush up on some common Irish terms before I got here."

"Ah, aren't you something!" Her big grin was

contagious. Over the next few minutes, we did find a "jacks" to freshen up in, then grabbed our bags, loaded up the trolley and headed out to this huge minivan. Thankfully it was roomy—we had a lot of luggage with us.

"Thank you so much for letting us stay in the family home. It's very generous of you," said Mia.

"Ah, sure look it! It was your Granda Leigh who went through all the trouble, ya know. It's the old O'Sullivan gaff down in Louisburgh. I'm up a bit a ways in Newport myself. No one actually be living there in Louisburgh at the moment. I have Mr. MacGovern tidying it up every week for me. Such a good man." She nodded in agreement with herself.

The view from the car was breathtaking—even if we were a bit unsettled driving on the opposite side of the road through millions of roundabouts. This place certainly earned its reputation as the Emerald Isle. The hills of such perfect greenery were like a painting, as we passed several pastures rotating between free range sheep, cows and horses along the way.

The depth of color was only heightened by the contrast of silver-clouded skies in the background. You would think that the rainy season would make it all dreary, but the lush green popped even more enchantingly like an emerald shining through a cave enclosure.

There was something so familiar about it. Like I had been here before. Almost as if I could take over the wheel and know exactly where I was driving. Such an odd sensation, since I had never been to Ireland—except in my dreams.

I know I have passed this landscape before, I ruminated in my head. I remember that goat farm in the distance, and that sharp curve in the road somehow. I even remember the debacle of having to reverse the car all the way up the road we just traveled on so a bus could pass on this narrow, one lane street. Déjà vu?

My trances along the trip were often interrupted by our dear cousin, who we quickly found out had a gift for gab. I mused to myself how she must have kissed the Blarney Stone many, many times.

"Now, where we be at now is in County Clare. That's where you'll be finding the touristy stuff. Are you planning on doin' some sightseein' at all?"

"Oh, yes! Definitely," squealed Marissa. "I want to explore as many ancient buildings as I can while I'm here and see art museums like the Hunt. I find that all so fascinating."

"I heard the Bunratty Castle has an extraordinary medieval dining experience that I signed us all up for," inserted Mia. "I booked an extra reservation for Saturday night if you'd like to join us, Colleen."

"That'd be fierce! I do love going on the lash!"

"Having a night out," I whispered to my perplexed sisters.

"So, you best be planning on stayin' down south for a spell. I have your spending money from Granda Leigh that should cover things like that. I'll be givin' that to ya when we get to the house.

"Where you'll be resting is in County Mayo. It originated from *Contae Mhaigh Eo*. That's Gaelic for 'plain of the yew trees.' It's a grand place. Right upon the Atlantic Ocean with its own treasures indeed. You might want to be checkin' out Croagh Patrick, too—that's an ancient pilgrimage site. Quite lovely.

"Oh and Clare Island," she continued without inhaling.

"I haven't been there in donkey's years but 'tis a grand sight. You just take the ferry crossing from Roonagh Pier. It is rumored to have been the home of the Pirate Queen Grace O'Malley, don'tcha know."

"It all sounds so wonderful, thank you! I am typing this into my phone so we remember."

Mia's affirmation made Colleen beam even brighter. What a kind, sweet woman she was. The remainder of the two-and-a-half hour drive to our destination was filled with similar conversations of where we "must go" all along the coast—that is, both western and eastern coasts. She had us taking a train cross-country to Dublin, warning us that we best not leave until we see the Guinness Storehouse.

When we arrived at the O'Sullivan home, it was that brief point in time right after sunset where you can see all the hues of the sun mix with the impending darkness of the evening sky. As we drove over the bridge and through the entrance, I noticed the town had an unusual setup. I never saw connected buildings mingling both homes and stores in a single unit before—at least, not outside of a city. Usually, I see either a storefront or series of townhouses. But there we were, in the heart of the town, learning that her dear friend Ellie Walsh lived in the light yellow house in between the post office and pharmacy.

Our family home happened to be situated around the corner, next to another home with a diner on the other side of it and a hotel across the street. Interesting, to say the least. It reminded me of a Monopoly board.

But the house was simply charming. A tan two-story unit with a light brown roof hovering over three shutterless windows and a lower floor bay window aside a cobalt blue front door. Since the home was situated on a corner, it boasted a lovely lush side garden, full of glorious bushes and flowers, most likely native to the area. I bet I'd find Mia here every morning.

Oh, yes. There was a small, white wood porch on the side, too, with just enough room for a single, weathered rocking chair. I could feel the years of work stress fade away just by looking at this serene place.

"You must be all flogged after such a long trip. I'll wet the tea and see what dear MacGovern rustled up for us for supper. Ah, grand! He left us his mum's lamb stew. I'll heat that up with some of this nice sliced pan here.

"Now, I'll be having a rest here with you all tonight and be making a hearty breakfast to welcome ya properly. I do have to crack on to Newport in the afternoon, so you won't have a car. It'd be best that you don't try driving on these Irish roads, now, with the left and the right being all mixed up and the troublin' roundabouts, as you Americans seem to think.

"You have a bit o' money, plenty to help with transportation, and I got a few chums that can help as well. You'll work it out," she assured us.

"Oh—make certain to stock up on some messages, ya hear? You don't want to be pissin' away your cash on eating out all the time. Plenty of tools right here in the kitchen for ya."

"Mia's on food duty. She is the family cook—her food is amazing!" Mia smiled at Marissa's compliment.

"Well, well, isn't that something? I'll be happy to sample whatever you cook up one of these days. For now, rest up. I'll take care of tonight's supper and then tomorrow we can chat some more. Oh, feck! I almost forgot to give you a tour."

After she put up the tea and set the stew for heating, she walked us around our new living quarters. It was just as darling on the inside as it was out, in an old-fashioned kind of way. The bottom floor was covered in old, tattered pine hardwood except the kitchen, which had a worn-out white tile with a few cracks here and there.

Alongside the living room wall was a built-in bookshelf housing an assortment of books, photographs and knick-knacks that must have dated back centuries. The taupe-painted walls were adorned with various Celtic totems and magnificent nature paintings that complemented the rich colors of the house. Further adding to its history was a gorgeous woven Celtic-designed throw rug in vibrant colors of green, rust and gold.

Off to the right side, like an L-shaped turn, was the "setting area," as she called it. This was a more cozy space, with a gray leather loveseat and two matching high-back arm chairs adorned with light blue velvety throw pillows and matching Irish woolen blankets.

The seating was arranged in a semi-circle fashion around the brick fireplace and solid wood mantle—certainly not the cheap fake gas fireplaces of modern times. Stacked alongside of it were freshly cut pieces of wood and cast-iron pokers.

Above the mantle was a fascinating painted portrait of a man and woman—and if I didn't know better, I'd swear I was practically looking at the male version of myself.

His hair was golden, a gentle mop of blonde curls that stopped right above his shoulders. Underneath a light gray suit jacket, he wore a royal blue collared shirt that highlighted his deep, penetrating blue eyes—I'd venture that they were even more vibrant than this decades-old painting could reveal. A matching light gray bowtie finished his ensemble—no, dare I say, his smile did, with the single dimple on his right cheek playfully revealing itself.

The woman beside him was just as lovely, with exotic chocolate wavy locks rolling down the sides of her face and curling at an end right above her breasts. Atop her head was a veil-like hat of white with small pink roses weaved into it. Her demure white lace blouse had beautiful pearls sown into the bodywork, all accentuating her beautifully Mediterranean skin tone and dark brown eyes.

Again, the familiarity struck me, as I could see our Mia in her reflection. In all her sweet rambling, Colleen had not revealed who they were, but I made a mental note to ask her when she was done with her stories.

Moving on past the setting area was the very small but functional combination kitchen and dining room. A solid dark pine wood table sat close to the edge of the wall with two matching benches on the long sides and two head chairs. The table set-up and centerpiece had a country feel to it—warm, welcoming and homely.

The yellow painted walls, pine colored cabinets and rustic decorations added to the country feel, offset by only a few modern touches of a granite countertop and relatively new white appliances. Off towards the back was a tiny room that she told us held a basic washer and dryer and some storage space.

At least we wouldn't have to wash our clothes on a washboard in a local stream, I joked to myself. That's how old this place appeared to be.

She stopped for a moment to brew our tea—never stopping her chatter, however. As it steeped, she led us up a narrow red-carpeted staircase by the front entrance that opened to a tiny hallway. Upstairs held a series of three bedrooms—one modest master and two relatively smaller rooms. I immediately called dibs on the master as the eldest, to my sisters' disappointment.

The master was a lovely shade of lilac with accenting floral curtains that made you feel like you were about to rest in a meadow. A queen-sized bed sat at the center of the room with a matching purple floral duvet ensemble and assortment of fluffy pillows in all shades of violet.

The dark mahogany bedpost was complemented with matching nightstands, dressers and a velvety lounge chair with a tall reading lamp. So cozy and inviting. The full-mirrored door inside opened to a long, deceivingly deep closet. Not the huge walk-in I was used to, but it would do for now.

Right outside of the hallway bathroom was a dangling string that presumably led to the attic…calling to me like a treasure map pointing to the big "X" marks the spot.

As Colleen ventured down to check on our dinner, we brought up our luggage and settled into our respective rooms. We took turns freshening up quickly and quietly, as we took it all in.

"Well now, don't you look all comfortable." Colleen greeted us with a beautiful bowl of steaming stew, glasses full of a local red wine and a teapot ready for post-dinner enjoyment. *Hmm,* I didn't realize how hungry I was.

"This is absolutely delicious!" Mia exclaimed. "My compliments to the chef!"

"Well, I won't be takin' any credit for that. Maybe if you see that Mr. MacGovern around here, you could be so kind as to let him know for his mum."

We continued dinner with some small talk, clearly feeling the drain of the day. We offered to help Colleen clean up the kitchen before settling down in front of a fire with a nice cup of Barry's Irish tea…and a few scones, of course.

"Colleen, who is that couple in the portrait?"

"Ah, now that would be your great-great grandparents, Cian and Alessia O'Sullivan," she said. "Quite the love story, ya know. Star-crossed lover stuff. But that would be a story for your ancestors in Italy to tell. We each were given our specific tales to tell you."

She lowered her voice in a frustrated aside. "Though I don't know why it has to be so prim and proper and all with the way of the tellin'.

"Here, you'll be learning about your great-great-great grandparents, Elena and Baran. There be much to say, but best be savin' it for another night. We've got plenty o'time."

She paused, but only for a moment. "You should be goin' up to rest your weary bones now. Like I said, I'll be gettin' up early in the mornin' to rustle up some breakfast before I'm on my way. We can chat some more then."

We all hugged good night and went up to our rooms. Colleen had already told us she planned on sleeping on the pull-out sofa, refusing to accept any of our offers to stay in one of our rooms for the night.

As the house went still, my mind started racing with questions. Star-crossed lover ancestors? Who were they really and why couldn't Colleen divulge any info? What story *was* she able to tell us? What should we do first— stay here and learn more about our heritage or explore like tourists? Why is everything so familiar to me?

After what seemed like hours of internal mental inquiries, I finally drifted off to sleep in the comfort of a home I somehow already knew.

When I finally woke up, the sun was bright and peeking in through the cracks of the blinds in the bedroom window. On top of my resistance to being an early bird, the jet lag made it even more difficult for me to turn over and check the time.

Ten o'clock? Wow, I guess I was more tired than I thought.

I took a few deep breaths as I gazed upon my surroundings, soaking up the nuances of the room that I missed in the evening light. My nose caught the scent of bacon and my stomach responded in turn. I would rather have lulled around under the covers until I felt ready to rise, but a hungry growl was pushing me out the door like an excited little puppy.

Down in the kitchen, my sisters were already up and chatting away with Colleen, who was setting the table with the last dish. As she removed her breakfast-stained, red-checkered apron, she was a vision in a bright yellow and green floral dress with flat loafer shoes.

"Perfect timing!" she exclaimed. "I just made the last of it. What's your fancy?"

"I'll just have some tea, thanks." I wasn't big on coffee. I just couldn't get used to the taste. My palate enjoyed a nice, relaxing cup of tea in the morning to get started. Though I did appreciate the smell of a freshly brewed pot of java.

From what I gathered, Mia was already on her third cup. She couldn't function without it and since she was probably up before the birds, it was a safe bet it wasn't her first go-round. Nope, already dressed with her hair done perfectly up in a bun, I'd say she'd been awake for quite a while.

Marissa was probably nursing her first cup—black. It was interesting how she would either drink just straight black coffee or fancy frappuccinos, but nothing in between. Like me, mornings were more challenging for her, as evidenced by her open robe and light pink silk nightie.

A breakfast feast welcomed us to the table: scrambled eggs, crisp bacon, pork sausages, a little unusual muffin-like thing I came to find out was black pudding (which didn't taste anything like pudding or a muffin), hash browns, fresh fruit, some rye toast and assorted jams and lemon-poppyseed scones. You'd think she was feeding an army with all this food.

"Everything looks delicious, Colleen. Thank you again for all your hospitality," I said.

"Ah, it be nothing, lass. Eat up now. I won't be 'round for another day or two, so you'll be on your own with the cookin'. I take it you slept well?"

"Oh, yes, thank you," said Mia. "This house is lovely. Very comforting."

"That's grand. Now I was thinkin' you should stay here at least one more night before you go out on the town," she said in her 'I have your itinerary all planned out' kind of way.

"I agree. I was planning on walking through the town, going to the market, things like that."

"Oh Meg, if I give you a list, would you mind picking up a few things for me for dinner? It's been so long since I have been without a husband or kids, I would really love to just stay here, sit on that side porch and read a book. It would be so nice to have a day without running any errands."

"Of course, Mi! I think that's a great idea. Mar, how about you?"

"If you don't mind, I was going to research some more places to check out while we are here, so we can talk about where we want to go and make a plan later. That cool? Or do you need help?"

"I think I can manage a few bags of groceries."

"This be a local town, so there won't be a trouble if you brought a basket home with you and returned it later. Not sure about the trolleys though. Best be bringin' some coins if you want for one of them. Ah, and in the cubby over there be some bags. Cost extra now if you don't bring some with you.

"Now, the Gala Market is in the center of town, about half a kilometer down the road on the left towards the bridge."

"Wonderful, thank you! I am excited to explore the town."

"Well, I'll be crackin' on now. You have my number in case you need to give me a ring. I already let them nosy neighbors know who's in here so they don't call the Garda on you. Though I suppose you should be prepared for some popover greetings from them. Grand crew, though. Lovely people.

"Enjoy your time here. Oh—and don't be worrying about no crickety sounds. That just be your relatives peeping in on ya from time to time. I reckon that cod brother o' mine Shane be curious to see who's shacking up here himself."

"Shane? Isn't he—" Marissa broke off midsentence as Colleen shot back a wink and left us on that note.

"Great, ghosts. That makes me want to take a shower right now," I said sarcastically as we shivered at the very idea of being in a haunted house.

A little freaked out about the thought of some dead cousin watching me undress, I jumped in and out of the shower, opting for piling my hair on top of my head in a wet, messy bun and throwing on a pair of faded blue jeans and the first sweater I saw—a light blue cashmere.

I kept the makeup light as I was on vacation and didn't see the need to get all dolled up for a walk to the market, especially since I was all bundled up under layers anyway. Just a touch of foundation and light mascara would do. With purse in hand, I was ready to go exploring.

The houses along our street were basically on top of each other, with nothing but a cement sidewalk as the front yard and little space for privacy. It reminded me of a city, yet with the quiet movement of the suburbs.

So much community. Kids playing ball in the backyards; families bringing in grocery bags from their parked cars; a big, burly man standing outside smoking a cigarette; and a nice elderly couple sitting together in their own side garden at the opposite end of the block— she was knitting and he was whittling wood.

No doubt everyone would know everyone else's business around here. As much as I was a private person myself, the thought of that neighborly closeness didn't bother me for some reason. *Strange,* I mused.

As I walked on, I came across the stretch of town that held most of the shops and very few homes. So many adorable window fronts—hand-woven rugs, knitted sweaters, whipped ice cream, Celtic jewelry, a pharmacy, a toy store, about four different pubs—I definitely need to come back down here just to investigate these little shops some more.

But first, I was on a mission to find the grocery store.

Ah, there it was. Nothing too different than the local little retailers I was used to, I suppose. I took Colleen's advice and went with a basket. I was only picking up a few items for a day or two until we had a game plan.

Stepping inside, it was like a farmers market with an abundance of fresh fruits and vegetables right up front. The shoppers were all so friendly, chatting with each other and sharing recommendations on this product or another. Just in a foreign language that was supposed to sound like English, I observed curiously. Accents are thicker than bacon around here.

There was such a peace and happiness to my new surroundings, though. Everything was easy and simple. Ha, simple. The exact opposite of my chaotic life. Since arriving, I've fought the urge to check my emails or return messages.

I had a few texts from Derek, but thankfully, by the end of the unreturned message thread, he had figured it out. Still, did he need me to double check the copy anyway? No. I told the team that I was going to be unreachable and I was going to keep that promise to myself to let this be my time. I deserved a break, damn it.

I've spent countless years and nights burning the midnight oil at that place. Picking up the slack for incompetent but cheaper staff members. Budget cuts can be such a nightmare.

Or maybe it really was my expectations. I set the bar

so high sometimes that even I can't reach it. But how else would we land such high-profile clients? "If you want something done right, you have to do it yourself." The motto of my clichéd life.

But now, in this moment, I had to choose to let go of the reigns and trust that my people were good enough to hold down the fort. Besides, if they don't do a great job, then that only validates how much I'm needed.

Holy shit. Did I really just think that?

Since when was I insecure about my job or my abilities? Is that why I chose all these years to work non-stop, so that I would make myself somehow irreplaceable?

What was going on at work right now? Maybe they were making changes while the control freak was gone. Am I going to come back to a completely altered career that no longer values me?

You're being ridiculous, Megan. Get a grip. You are a hard worker and good at what you do. They can get by without you, but they thrive with you. Let it go and—

Smack!

Lost in conversation with myself, I didn't notice anyone behind me as I backed up looking for the carrots Mia requested.

"Oh my goodness, I am so—" I looked up, stunned at the gorgeous man in front of me, barely mumbling out, "Sorry."

"Not a worry, miss," he said in a sexy brogue. Before me stood a 6-foot tall deity with a handsomely chiseled face. He was like a work of Irish art with his long, raven hair that waved just above his shoulders, his green-blue gaze and some dark stubble around his broad chin.

He was sporting ripped jeans and a green, blue and white flannel over a dirtied white t-shirt. His entire essence oozed sex appeal like I imagined a Celtic God would.

And this is why you should always put makeup on before going out, Megan, I chided myself.

"Are you alright?" he broke my nomadic thoughts, which were probably written all over my face as I continued to stare at this poor man like a psychopath.

"What? Oh, yes. Yes, sorry. I'm—grand," I managed to respond, as I nervously fussed with my hair—as if I could make a messy bun look fabulous.

"Grand, are ya?" He had a hearty, yet pleasant enough laugh that I could imagine was contagious. Well, it sucked me in. "So, an American lass is tryin' on some Irish, is she now?"

I blushed. Blushed? Oh my God, what is wrong with me? I've never turned to jelly in front of a man like this before. I'm an empowered, independent woman!

Buck up Megan, before he thinks you are a complete idiot, I warned myself.

"Well, when in Rome," I said, lamely attempting a joke, though judging by his confused face, I'm pretty sure the Irish aren't familiar with that saying. "I'm Megan. I'm here with my sisters visiting a cousin and this is my first time in town."

"Well, *céad míle fáilte*, Miss Megan. A thousand welcomes," he winked as he extended his hand to shake mine. Who ordered the lightning bolt? "I'm Kieran. And who might your cousin be?"

"Colleen O'Sullivan." His eyes raised in recognition and his lips in a semi-smirk.

"Do you know her?"

"Lassie, this is a small town. Everybody knows everybody around here. Colleen O'Sullivan happens to be one of my favorite old mots. A darlin', she is. Chatty little nugget, but as kind as they come. How long will you be staying?"

"Well, we are here for a few weeks. My grandfather, who I didn't even know was a grandfather, left us this mysterious will about traveling to three countries to find our heritage and I'm supposed to get some kind of ring here, which I know nothing about and—"

I looked up to see an amused expression on his face. Oh God, I was rambling—and rambling about something that was supposed to be a family secret.

What the hell, Meg?

"I'm sorry, I'm going on and on and probably boring you to tears."

"On the contrary. I'm finding our conversation fascinating. A secret granda and mysterious ring? It's the stuff storybooks are made of. Lucky you for getting to live it."

"I guess so." Awkward silence passed, as I tried my hardest not to stare into his swimming pool eyes. I didn't realize they even made men this perfect anymore. And something about that accent was making me weak in the knees, like some high school girl whose crush just said "hi" as he walked past her locker.

"Well, I best be on my way. My mum's waitin' on me to bring her some messages. It was grand meeting you, though I dare say my left foot mighta been a bit bruised in our scuffle." He chuckled warmly.

"Sorry again. It was nice to meet you too, Kieran." I succeeded to even more awkwardly put out my hand to shake it, secretly hoping to feel the electricity again. To my surprise, he lifted my hand up to his lips and gave it a gentle kiss with his soft, thick lips as he stared straight into my eyes—into my soul.

"I'm sure to be seein' you again, Miss Megan." And off he went, stopping once to turn his head around and smile as I stood there, lifeless.

Thank goodness Mia had written everything down that we needed because I felt like I just had a lobotomy. I was complete mush. Jeez, how long has it been since I'd been with a man?

Oh right, just a few months ago I had ended it with Eddie Birkens, an associate in our sister organization that I met at a recent trade show in Vegas. Nothing happened in Vegas since we were professionals, but the second we got back to New York, the sex was on. It was a good tumble for a few months, but it wasn't meant to be much more than that.

I got bored—and not because he wasn't attractive or because we didn't have great physical chemistry, but I was left wanting more. Although a well-respected peer, he lacked the level of intellectual stimulation I required in an ongoing relationship. I need someone not afraid to challenge my mind, and he was a man of very few words and insights.

Running into this Kieran guy was more than that. It was a spark I hadn't felt since my first long-term relationship in my twenties. Back then, I thought Scotty and I would have been married with a few kids by now.

Unfortunately, his wandering dick squashed that delusion and I resolved instead to put my whole heart into my job. Sure, there were a few decent men along the way, not all straight-up sex, but none had been the right one for me. No one compared to Scotty or to the feelings that I had for him. He was my one and only prince-charming-gone-wrong.

The man who single-handedly ruined the girlish

notions of romance for me.

Yet, one single encounter with Kieran seemed to stir that all up. My stomach fluttered and my heart raced. How is that possible? I just met the guy and barely talked to him. More like rambled at him. I can't explain these funky emotions—just like I can't explain the familiarity of Ireland. I felt instantly drawn to him as if I had already known him.

And I just let that man walk away.

Would I ever see him again? I wondered. *What is going on with you, Meg?* I had to shake off all this drivel. Setting my head back on straight, I finished my task at hand and gathered up our groceries—all while occasionally looking around to see if I could spot my new Irish crush again.

He vanished as quickly as he showed up. But his musky scent and sparkling eyes accompanied me as I walked back to the O'Sullivan house.

When I arrived, Mia was relaxed with her cute red reading glasses on, sitting in the rocking chair, completely submerged in her book. Marissa was chatting away on her phone near the garden of white lilies in the back of the house and hurriedly said goodbye to whoever she was talking to as she saw me approach.

"Who was that?"

"Oh, it's just Jay. Checking in on us," she replied a little too quickly. I'm guessing by now their relationship had crossed that line—I mean, he *really was* one sexy guy. I wouldn't be able to resist him. No use in pressing her for details, though. We'll find out as soon as it's over. "How was the market?"

"Interesting. It was difficult to find everything because my logic didn't seem to match up with theirs. But it was adorable and friendly, just like the rest of this town. You should check it out with me next time. There were some great little shops I saw where we could get some souvenirs for Mom and Granny and Kevin and the kids."

I decided to leave out my interlude with Kieran for now. I needed time to recover from my out of body experience. No, correction—to put it behind me because it was one of those one-time-only destined moments. No use even bringing it up. I'll just tuck it away in one of my private memory archives.

"So, Mia, what are your plans for all this stuff I got for you?"

"I was thinking of trying my hand at shepherd's pie. It's a simple dish to make and easy enough to have for leftovers tomorrow so I won't have to cook every night."

"That's smart. This is your vacation as much as ours and even though we'd love to be spoiled with your cooking, we need to be fair about it."

"I agree with Marissa. Maybe we should come up with some kind of chore chart. I mean, we will be staying here in this home and need to upkeep it and feed ourselves. If we all rotate some meals and clean-up, we can make sure it's fair. And since Marissa and I are better suited for breakfast and lunch duty than dinner, we can take some nights off from home-cooked meals and dine out in style, thanks to our grandfather's little trust fund."

"Brilliant idea. Why don't you take care of organizing that? I'm good with whatever you assign me," said Mia.

"Me too. And while you work on that, I am finishing up a sightseeing plan for us. I have some really cool ideas on how to fit it all in. I, too, can be a wonderful organizer," Marissa declared with pride.

"Perfect. Let's get to work and then talk about it over dinner tonight."

I did everything I could to pull a chart together, but between my wandering mind and the glorious kitchen smells, I was easily distracted. I could still see those exquisite baby blues looking at me with great humor. I felt the rush of embarrassment flush back into my cheeks in recollection of my girlish reaction.

What was it about this international lad that made me instantly giddy? This is not how a professional Senior VP acts! Where was my composure?

It didn't matter anyway. It's not like I'm going to see him again. I'm not one to really believe in all that destiny and serendipity crap. Like that was some kind of love at first sight moment and we would magically meet up again, fall in love and live happily ever after.

Grow back up, Megan. Get real.

Oh, who am I kidding? Deep down in my soul, as much as I resist it, I am a sucker for romance. Fine, I admit that when I am alone on the weekends, I watch those diabetically sweet and predictable television chick flicks and secretly wish for the iconic love story to enter my own life.

Thanks to my idyllic cable addiction, the idea of running into this beautiful stranger again in such a small town ignites fireworks in my soul. For too long I have suppressed the inner romantic in me, living in the reality of a man's world and jaded by the decline of gentlemen in my path.

I let my imagination wander about how it would feel to be held in those super strong arms and touched by those manly hands. Kissed by those full, satiable lips.

I could write a novel about this kind of once-in-a-lifetime experience. American girl meets Irish boy and he changes her life. She gives up her ambitious, corporate ways to choose love over power and prestige. Classic tale, but like all stories, they can be recreated with unique twists and turns. Before I knew it, I somehow had my laptop open and just started composing.

It had been years since I let myself write something other than a business report or ad proposal. A lifetime ago, I would have indulged in imaginative prose that brought me laughter and joy. It was a passion I subdued in pursuit of a better life for myself; one in which I could provide a solid foundation that I could be proud of.

But what had I sacrificed along the way? And why am I all of a sudden questioning my life decisions?

My queries were interrupted by the call to come to dinner. Quickly finishing up our chore distribution, I made my way down the creaky stairs.

"I found so many places that we can explore over here on the west coast," began Marissa, while I stepped in to help Mia serve what was undoubtedly going to be a fantastic dinner.

"I think our best bet is to sign up for one of these guided bus tours down the southwest coast," she continued. "It's five days long but will cover hot spots like the Cliffs of Moher, Galway City, the Hunt Museum, historic abbeys and the Blarney Castle. A little something for each of us."

"Five days is an awfully long time to just travel when we only have two weeks. We're here on a mission," Mia reminded her. I couldn't help but laugh—even now, she was such a mom.

"Yes, but I spoke with Colleen earlier today and she will be tied up for quite a few days. Something unexpected came up with her other cousins up in Newport and she told me we should do the tourist thing now," Marissa explained.

"If we are unable to get any answers, we might as well take advantage of this opportunity in front of us. I worked it out where if we leave tomorrow, we'll end up by the Bunratty Castle for our dinner on Saturday and Colleen can meet us out there. At that point, we can wrap up our trip and head back with her."

"I think that sounds like great plan, Mar. We could all use the brainless activity before we get into whatever it is that really brought us here. I'm in!"

Mia looked up from serving the steaming shepherd's pie onto the dishes and smiled at us. "Okay then, count me in, too!"

We all turned to each other with a group high five, ready to take on Ireland.

7

Ireland was every bit as breathtaking as we imagined. Our first stop was in Connemara, known for representing true authentic Ireland heritage. On the border of counties Mayo and Galway, the wild, untamed landscapes were a vision to behold.

Here we experienced Killary Harbour, Ireland's only fjord. We opted for the 90-minute boat tour around the majestic scenery. Words could hardly describe the beauty of the countryside, which ebbed and flowed in an incredible range of colors—between the lush green hills, the naturally carved glacial shale stone edges and the glistening of the water.

We met a lovely couple, Eric and Daniel, who were from California and celebrating their honeymoon. Together we dined on the native mussels that were farmed from the harbor as we gleefully spotted a few otters and seals playing hide and seek in the water.

After our sea excursion, we indulged in the land's perspective of the harbor by taking a pony trek around the beaches and hills of Connemara. Although we were not avid horse riders, thankfully our ponies were mild and tame as they skillfully took us on a gorgeous seaside expedition.

It was a dream come true. Whoever would have thought in a million years that we would have a rich grandfather who would want us to indulge in this kind of life experience? As I breathed in the views, I no longer felt guilty for doing so; I felt immense gratitude.

After spending the night at a traditional little bed and breakfast in a nearby fishing village, we ventured on further south with a stopover in the cultural destination of Galway City. We instantly fell in love with its artistic charm, which held a different intrigue for each of us.

I adored a medieval walking tour honoring historic Galway; Marissa was mesmerized by the Spanish Arch; and Mia couldn't get enough of the street markets and musicians as we tasted our way through the city.

We ended up at the iconic Cliffs of Moher a few hours before sunset, stumbling upon the most stunning vista I have ever witnessed in my entire life. We hiked up the South Platform, where we were able to see the acclaimed puffin colony on Goat Island and a strikingly clear panoramic view of O'Brien's Tower at the opposite side of the cliffs.

Fueled with energy and awe, we trekked on towards Hag's Head. There, up against the jagged edges of one of the resplendent cliffs overlooking the Atlantic Ocean, I could feel several lifetimes merging at once. The memory of it all blasted at me as hard as the winds that nearly knocked us over the cliff.

The magic in the air was undeniable. Rushing back to me were the ancient myths I remembered reading about when I was younger, during a time when I was so enthralled by everything Celtic. I'd read book after book about the legends and deities associated with the Emerald Isle.

At this very spot, it was said that the Tuatha Dé Danann fled on horse and fell over the edge, dubbing this the Leap of the Foals. Then there was the story about a fisherman who discovered and fell in love with a mermaid here. Or, my personal favorite, how beneath the sea sits the Lost City of Kilstiffen, a kingdom that is said to return to its former glory once the golden key to the castle is found. I felt equally lost as I felt found right here in this very spot.

"Meg, are you okay?" Mia asked, breaking the silence. I had no idea that in my daydream, tears had started streaming faintly down my cheeks. I brought my finger up to touch one as I turned to face my two sisters.

"Oh! I guess I was so touched by it all, I hadn't even noticed I was crying! This place is just so—spellbinding. I feel like it isn't even real."

"I feel the same way. It's like you are transported to another space and time," Marissa agreed.

"Yeah. Exactly. I mean—this is going to sound odd. But do either of you feel like you have been here before?"

Marissa and Mia quickly exchanged puzzled looks. "Not really," said Marissa. "Why, do you?"

"Yes, and I can't explain it. I know it's crazy. But I feel this sense of home, this air of peace, being here in Ireland. It's the complete opposite of everything I am, all the hustle and bustle of a corporate life, always on the go. All of this makes me just want to stop and—I don't know—breathe it all in. Like all of this is enough."

"I don't think it's the complete opposite of everything you are, Meg," replied Mia, as she reached out to touch my arm. "I've known you all your life, remember? You are a strong girl with a tough outer shell of ambition, but you've hidden your true self behind that.

"The Megan I know inside is the sister who had a vivid imagination and who would write the most wild stories as a child. She stargazed with Daddy about exploring unknown worlds and loved storybook fantasies. The woman who doesn't even realize it, but purposely lives outside of the city and commutes because she can't live 24/7 in that crazy urban vibe."

She paused a moment, unsure of whether or not to continue her retrospect, but decided to do so soothingly.

"I know Scotty hurt you. I know you thought that you would spend your fairy tale life with him. When that jackass broke your heart, the only way you knew how to survive was to become tough. Don't you think it's time to let that hurt go and allow the inner Megan to come back out? Maybe that's why you feel at home here. Because when I see all of this, I see *you*."

I sunk down to the ground, the waterworks falling endlessly in hearty sobs as my sisters gathered around me and held me until I could weep no more. Mia knew me better than I knew myself.

Scotty had plunged a hole in my heart that I hardened and blocked through a career. Work never disappointed. I thrived at my job. There, no one could hurt me or take me down because I knew my worth. They'd never let me go because I was too valuable. They'd never replace me.

Or would they? Here I was in the stunning country of Ireland and one of the first anxieties to pop into my head was, what if they could carry on without me? What if they found out I *was* replaceable?

Scotty thought I was. He had no problem moving on with Bethany, marrying her within six months of us breaking up and starting the family I envisioned having with him.

Oh God, have I really been carrying this inside of me all this time? Did I turn myself into a workaholic not for power or prestige, but so that I wouldn't feel?

The realization clobbered me like a baseball bat to the head. I had given up my passion of writing because it would stir up emotions that I needed to keep buried. I cut myself off from the world and from love so I couldn't feel that pain ever again.

It was so overwhelming to bear this all at once. I had felt bits and pieces emerging ever since we landed, but in the solitude of the present moment, I was forced to face the entire puzzle of my life, whether I wanted to or not. The pain was being exorcised and I had no control.

I had no control.

That frightened me even more than heartbreak. I was all about control. I decided when, where, how. Emotions included. But now I was as vulnerable as I'd ever been in my life. I felt broken, the glass within me shattering. Completely fragmented.

"Oh Meg, I am so, so sorry. I should not have been so blunt. I don't know what came over me," Mia expressed regretfully as she sat alongside me.

"Please don't apologize, little sis." I squeezed her and Marissa's hands lightly. "You were only trying to help. And you were right. Everything you said was true. I have been suppressing it for so long that it had to be said. God, what a horrible sister I must have been this last decade."

"Eh, we got used to it," Marissa joshed. "But in all seriousness, I get it. Love is hard. We grew up watching a real-life Cinderella story in Mom and Dad, and for you and me, it hasn't panned out like that. I know Scotty really did a number on you, but he did it to us, too. He was like a brother to me and for him to walk out on all of us dealt a blow that I haven't quite recovered from either."

I looked up at her with a compassion I haven't had in years. I had such a low tolerance for this sister who was so unlike me, only now to realize that we have the same heart after all; we simply expressed our grief in different ways. I reached out and embraced her.

"I'm so sorry, Mar."

"It's okay. Maybe this is what we needed. Maybe this is what the trip is really about. Sure, you might get some cool ring at the end of this, but like we questioned before, it could have easily been shipped to us. Or you could have traveled here to recover it on your own, while Mia went to Italy and I went to Spain.

"We were meant to travel together on this adventure—an adventure designed to bring us closer together. Maybe even learn more about ourselves and support each other along the way. Maybe Grandfather Leigh really did have an inkling into who we were and what we needed in order to become the women we were meant to be—and Ireland is your place to discover you."

"That is uncharacteristically deep of you," I joked to break the uncomfortable heaviness of the moment as she rolled her eyes. "Kidding. I know how smart you are, Mar. And it's true. There is definitely more to this journey than an heirloom and a mystery."

"I'm just glad that you are the one to go first!" she countered.

With a burst of giggles, my sisters helped me up off the ground. We linked hands in an unbreakable bond, walking back down the cliffs as the sun set into gorgeous streams of red, orange and yellow.

As everyone from our group began the walk back to the bus, I asked my sisters to go on and leave me for a moment. I stood there in that mystical place, closing my eyes and taking a vow.

Here, I will leave behind the pain of the past. Here, I

will release my broken heart and melt the ice that keeps the warmth away. Here, I will say goodbye to the dream of Scotty, who was not meant to be mine, and say hello instead to future love. Here, I will let the shell of control-freak Megan go and set my true self free.

It's time to honor who I am and fearlessly live the life I was meant to.

"A round of pints for everyone!" shouted Marissa, as she plopped down a wad of cash on the beer-soaked pub counter. Turning to us with pints of Guinness, she gleefully declared, "Tonight, we have earned the right to get knackered!"

It only took us four days before finally getting ourselves to an authentic pub. After the long, emotional day, I was certainly grateful for the change in atmosphere and some brain numbing. The music and crowd were lively and loud, as was expected for an Irish tavern.

Beer was splashing, laughter was roaring all around and people were dancing and cheering like life was the grandest thing on earth. It was hard not to fall into the easygoing charm of it all.

"What should we drink to?" Mia asked.

"Living in the moment," I responded.

They nodded their heads in agreement and with a raising of the glasses, we exclaimed, "To living in the moment!"

We found a somewhat quiet little corner nook to settle down with our beers and order some food, since we were absolutely starving. I decided on classic fish and chips, while Mia delighted in ordering an oak grilled salmon and Marissa a burger—which she never had a chance to eat because she ended up dancing with some hot Irishman who was bedazzled by her exotic looks.

Before we knew it, she was running over to let us know what room she was going to be staying in that night—instead of with us—and warned us to make sure to get her in the morning before the bus left. *Ah, Marissa.*

Left alone with Mia, we enjoyed our meal while being surrounded by the liveliness of the scene. Oh how we relished the dancing, the drinking and the jolly good cheer of contagious laughter. The Irish really know how to live in joy, and it was inspiring.

I hoped that I could keep my vow to let that part of me back out. But I could feel the weight of the emotional release taking a toll on my energy level and knew I wouldn't be able to hold out much longer. My battery was draining quicker than a car whose headlights were left on.

"You know, I really am sorry I said all that earlier. But I am glad that I was able to see a glimpse of the old Meg back there. I just want to see you happy again."

"I know. I do, too. When you went back to the bus, I stood there and made a promise to myself to let go of past hurts and open my heart again. There's just something about this place that makes it seem easier to do than when I'm home."

"That's good! And who knows, maybe you will be the next one to meet a sexy Irishman!"

"Well…" I broke off, not meaning to drop the hint, but in my fatigued, alcohol-induced state, it just came out.

"Megan! What do you mean, 'well?'"

"Well…okay. I didn't really want to tell you guys about it, because it was nothing. It's so silly, really. Not exactly like taking off for a tumultuous night of passion like Marissa just did."

"Oh shut it, Meg and tell me!"

"Okay, okay! You win." I took a deep breath—why was I so nervous about telling the story?

"When I went down to the market the other day, I ran into this really good-looking local—literally, as in I ran over his foot. Oh my gosh Mia, he was absolutely dreamy, like out of a Gaelic *GQ Magazine*. I don't remember the last time a man made me so nervous!

"I was trying to figure out where everything was and I ended up backing into him. I then fumbled all my words and couldn't speak. Me, speechless! Imagine that."

"Uh, actually, I can't. Wow—so what happened?"

"I managed to get out a few audible words as these piercingly magnificent eyes stared right through me. Mia, I can't even describe it—I felt like I was back in high school when Scotty first walked by, but even more intense. Plus, he was funny and kind and made me feel comfortable even in all my gibberish."

"Ooh, sounds sexy. So, did you get his name? Are you going to see him again?"

"His name is Kieran. I highly doubt I'll ever randomly run into him again. Plus, he's probably married or has a girlfriend, anyway. It was just some chance encounter at the market and memories to keep me warm for a few days. That's all.

"But it was really nice to feel butterflies again. I haven't felt that in a while. It's what placed me onto this emotional rollercoaster of mixed feelings right now."

"Okay, so we need to go back and find this Kieran fellow then. Meg, you can't just give up!"

"Don't be silly. What am I going to do, track down every Kieran in the country until I find the right one? I can't get caught up in silly impulsive illusions."

I held my hand up before she could speak. "No. I can't do that to myself right now. There is a difference between me realizing that I need to heal the past and open back up for love versus going on a wild goose chase after a mystery man I just met."

"Okay, fine. But would it hurt for you to explore the men here in the meantime? You don't need to worry about me. Go out and enjoy yourself tonight."

"Thanks, but I'm not in the mood. There's more to what I'm feeling than casual sex. I don't want a random fling anymore that leaves my heart cold long after he leaves my bed. I actually want to meet someone sincere for a change. Like I'd rather have no one instead of a wrong one. Know what I mean?"

"Actually, I do." She said, kind of pensively. Now is my chance to dig deep and find out what was up with her before we were all interrupted that Sunday evening.

"Hey, we've been talking so much about me on this trip that I haven't asked how you've been doing."

"I'm fine. You know, same old."

"No Mia, don't pull that shit with me. Do you really think I didn't notice your mood before Joshua Perkins knocked on your door and dropped this mystery on us? Spill it. What's going on with you?"

"Nothing really. Just frustrated with Kevin always being out of the house with his new promotion and training. I mean, I am happy for him, of course, but I'd be lying if I said I wasn't a little bit jealous."

"Have you given any thought to opening up your restaurant like you always wanted to?"

"I have, but not sure what good thinking about it will do me. With Kevin out of the house so much now, the kids rely on me even more to get them back and forth to color guard and soccer and math tutoring and all that. I barely have time to read a book, let alone think about starting a new business. I just don't think it's in the cards for me."

"Why not? Why should you have to put your life on hold forever? The kids are older now—surely there are carpools you can get involved in or they can Uber to where they need to go."

Mia rolled her eyes at the mere thought of the children being inconvenienced in any way. "Yeah, right. As if!"

"Well, if there is anything I can do to help, just let me know. I'm here for you."

"I know and I appreciate that. There is just a lot I need to work through. It's not just the restaurant thing. I've actually come to terms with that. It's just that I'm feeling more and more like a single mom instead of a married woman." I couldn't believe she was opening up like this—that this was repressed inside her all this time. God bless Guinness. Why do we do this to ourselves?

"I do everything to keep the house running and my family satisfied, but no one is around to spend any time with me. Like I'm just their servant. The kids are always out with their friends or at after school programs and Kevin is always working. I can't even remember the last time we spent a night together."

She looked up at me as the embarrassment rushed to her face. My heart was breaking for her.

"I'm so sorry, Mi. I had no idea things had gotten so bad. I guess I'm just so absorbed in my own little world, and imagine you and Kevin have this perfect life, that I don't check in with you enough." I reached for her with a big bear hug.

"I'm really sorry and I am going to do better. Anything I can do for you?"

"No, but thank you. I really needed this trip. I didn't grasp how much I did until I got here. I am so glad you all pushed me to go. Maybe I can find myself again like you are finding yourself."

"No doubt you will. We are all in this together. Have you talked to Kevin about this—about how you feel?"

"I try, but he is always so exhausted when he gets home that he just wants to eat and go to bed. It's like I need to make an appointment with my own husband to even ask, 'How was your day?'"

"Well, maybe when you get back, you should insist on taking a day for you both to spend together. I'll volunteer to run the kids wherever they need to go and you both can just go out on a date and talk."

She smiled big. "I might just take you up on that offer. I think we would both like that.

"Okay," she added. "Enough about our sorrows. Let's grab another drink and get out on that dance floor before we call it a night, shall we?"

Early the next morning, we met up with Marissa at the bus and the smirk on her face told us all we needed to know. She wasn't too forthcoming with the details, but she did say she enjoyed her night and that she was easily falling in love with Ireland.

That love was deepened the moment we stepped off the bus and onto the pavement in front of the Hunt Museum in Limerick—flood lights couldn't compare to the brightness in her eyes. Her enthusiasm was contagious as she lovingly dragged us from exhibit to exhibit, oo-ing about the European medieval statues and ah-ing over ancient Egyptian artifacts.

Then came the squeals of delight as she entered the worlds of Picasso, Renoir and Moore; she could have stayed in there for hours looking at a single painting. Although art is not my thing, I did find myself in awe of the grandiose masterpieces that stood before me. Such heartfelt innovations preserved with such care.

The tour of the museum wouldn't have been complete without a stop in the gift shop to purchase a few framed prints that would look great in her living room, a series of Picasso cards and an oversized ceramic mug for her morning coffee. After grabbing a quick snack, we headed back to the bus to continue south to County Cork.

Since there is so much to do and not enough time for us to dig deep into everything we wanted to see, we decided to stick to either the classic touristy places or indulge in a unique experience. So in Cork, instead of seeing more museums, we opted to take a few smaller excursions throughout the city to encounter the culture.

With tons of energy, we started off with Mia's choice of exploration—a four-hour walking tour through the English Market, where we tasted our way through the city with cheeses, fresh oysters from the Atlantic Bay and sinfully-rich chocolates. We ended the jaunt with a full gourmet meal and local brew, which left us completely stuffed, but happy.

It didn't take much for Marissa to then nudge us onto a quick beer and whiskey tour, where we witnessed the brewing process and enjoyed world class samplings.

Although the amount of food we ate diminished our energy into a walking coma, I guilted my sisters into joining me on a fun ghost story evening stroll through an old part of town. Nothing like spooky tales to get you ready for bed—especially those laced with a bit o' truth (or so they say).

By day four of our journey, we were starting to feel the fatigue from being on-the-go so much, but how could we not absolutely love all that we were experiencing? Today was declared "castle day"—one I was very much looking forward to. The itinerary called for a tour of the Blarney Castle in the morning and then the long trip back up to Bunratty Castle for dinner.

Blarney holds such rich history and legend. The moment I began walking through the Garden of the Seven Sisters, I was enchanted. I didn't expect to ever be so fond of a single place on earth.

I was especially drawn to the lore of the witch who was said to inhabit the Rock Close area of the castle grounds. Rumor claims she is trapped within the large stone alongside her kitchen, tasked with granting the wishes of those who travel up and down her bewitched stairs. As a sucker for legends and magic, I took on the dare by my sisters to re-enact the wishing ritual.

I walked all the way up and then, quite awkwardly, all the way down the stairs backwards with my eyes closed, focusing only on the silly old desire of my childhood: to meet my own prince charming and live happily ever after.

Smiling at the thought, I winked at the bottom of the stairs as a challenge to the witch to bring forth my intention within the next year. I knew that it wasn't possible, but it was a nice change of pace to allow myself to be so innocently lighthearted. I could stand to lose some of my seriousness.

The energy of the ancient witch and Druid lore was all around. Exploring the different areas, we came upon the eerie Druid Cave, colorful Fairy Glade, the creepy Sacrificial Altar and the legendary Witch Stone, where I placed a few pennies in homage, as I wished for her own release. I could have sworn her apparition swirled around me in a ghostly hug.

We then walked through part of the majestic gardens, which could only be touched upon in the short amount of time we had left to spend there. We decided to stick to the Bog Garden area, enjoying the views of its two waterfalls, 600-year-old yew trees and a willow tunnel at the end of the path's boardwalk. I could tell this was where Mia wanted to venture for hours.

I didn't even know this kind of beauty existed in this world. There was so much more to see, but not enough hours to see it all.

We ended our time at the castle with—you guessed it—the climb up the steps to the infamous Blarney Stone. Now, there was no way that I was going to lean backwards over an edge (even if now safely enclosed with an iron railing) to touch my mouth to that bacteria-festering icon, but Marissa was game.

We encouraged her to go for it, as out of all of us, she was the one who could certainly use the promised gift of eloquence. That comment got me a playful punch as she conceded in agreement.

A light picnic lunch in the gardens ended our time in County Cork before we began the over four-hour trip back up towards Bunratty Castle. It was an unusually tranquil ride for us. Marissa had fallen asleep, Mia was reading her book and I found myself staring out of the window in reflection of all that had happened over just a few short days.

Mostly, I was in awe of how serene I felt. How at home I was. How enraptured by everything I had just witnessed in my mini circuit of this beautiful country. I could feel the magic in my veins, coursing through like a moonlit lake of fairy dusted potion.

Something in the air had awakened the essence of my soul and it called to me to play. My inner child couldn't help but want to run out in the middle of a meadow and sing; to stop and smell the unique perfumes of the flowers; or to write stories about the forbidden romance locked within the history of the castle ruins. Without my laptop on me, I settled for a journal I had in my bag and just let the words flow through me.

We arrived at Bunratty Castle just before sunset. It was as glorious a fortress as I could have ever imagined—right out of one of the childhood books Mom used to read to me. Structurally sound and well preserved, it was hard to believe that this was originally built in the early 1200's.

Oh, I just couldn't wait to get in there and experience the food and the music—and the renowned honey mead. What a great way to end our first little trip.

My thoughts were interrupted by Marissa's phone ringing. A few moments later, she rejoined us.

"That was Colleen. She'll be here soon—she's running just a bit behind. She's bringing a friend so she didn't have to drive up alone, which delayed her a bit. I already worked out an extra ticket, so that's taken care of."

"Oh, I'm glad. I was a bit worried about her making the trip. Though I suppose she is a pretty strong woman who can take care of herself," said Mia.

We walked over the stone drawbridge towards the Irish palace, checking in at the entrance and sneaking a peek at the neighboring gift shop. We then were escorted through the gardens to the castle itself, where we patiently waited outside as instructed until Colleen and her friend could join us.

I was overwhelmed with the historical architecture of this ancient structure and imagined what it would have been like to grow up as a princess in these halls. What marvelous balls they might have held. What scandals lived within the walls. A few minutes later, my reverie was broken by the excited babbling of our beloved cousin right behind us.

"Well, if this isn't a wonderful sight! Blessed be! Did you all have a grand time? I'm delira ta hear about all of it!" We all stepped in to hug and kiss her, excitedly starting to talk over each other about our favorite parts of our expedition, not noticing her friend coming up from behind.

"So, these must be the American cousins you have told me all about," he interrupted in introduction. My heart stopped instantly—I knew that voice.

"Feck, I am such an eejit! Forgive me my manners. Yes, this be Marissa, Mia and Megan, though I still have difficulty sometimes rememberin' which is which. Cousins, this lad here be my good friend, Kieran MacGovern," she said fondly. "He be our prince charmin' tonight, that he will."

With a wickedly playful smile that showed off his chiseled cheekbones, he turned to take my hand to raise it up to his soft lips and kiss it before bringing those extraordinary eyes back up to meet mine. "Hello again, Miss Megan."

With one look, I immediately felt starstruck and at home all at once. If ever there was a time to believe in Irish folklore, this was it. *Damn, that Blarney witch worked fast.*

"""A"""y, so you know each other already? Fancy that! What's the story?" asked Colleen, as our entire audience watched us, locked in the moment like a frozen computer screen.

Still in shock, I was grateful that Kieran answered for us.

"We met the other day down by the market, when she backed up and over my foot with the trolley," he chuckled in remembrance, which only made me fluster even more.

"I'm so sorry, again," I managed. "How is your foot?"

"I'm no worse for the wear, lass."

"Would ya get outta that garden! Kieran, ya real cute hoor. All this time ye be knowin' Miss Megan would be here and you never let on? Quite the clever man, this one is. Is that why you was slyly askin' about whether me cousins were taken or not?"

Now it was his turn to flush slightly. Colleen was not one for subtlety, that's for certain. Did he really know I would be here? Did he come to see *me?*

I wanted to throw up. Thankfully, Mia stepped in to rescue us all from the awkward silence.

"Colleen, why don't you come with me up the stairs to the Green Hall? I bet you know the best spot to view the pre-show. Marissa, why don't you head up first to make sure the stairwell is clear?" she hinted.

Marissa started to protest, but then caught the glare of her older sister beckoning her to join them. With a confused look back up at me and Kieran, she obliged, though I could hear the questioning whispers as they walked away.

I looked up to see Kieran smiling down at me. I didn't realize how even a few inches could make a man appear so much taller, towering over me like the Empire State Building.

"I believe I told you I'd be seein' you again."

"Did you really know I'd be here?"

"I did. When Colleen told me all about your little adventure to the castle and then droned on about how she had to drive up here all by her lonesome, I offered to accompany her. I'm sorry if I've made you uncomfortable, *a ghrá*."

My love? The Irish sure were friendly and free with their endearments. And yet, it made me melt faster than global warming.

"No, not at all. Just—surprised. I didn't think we'd ever meet again." Something about his name sounded familiar though, I realized. "MacGovern? I've heard that name before."

"MacGovern I am. I'm after taking care of the house you are stayin' in. Perhaps you heard a bit about my mum's cookin', too."

"Yes, that's it! So that explains why you knew Colleen when I mentioned her and were so confident you would see me again. And here I thought it was some kind of destiny," I teased.

His laid-back mannerisms made it easy to begin to relax around him. The edginess I felt was slowly dissolving away into a sense of comfort.

"Maybe it *is* destiny," he replied, looking back at me intently—my comfort slowly fading away again. How can anyone have this kind of intensity in a single look? It could inspire the earth to rumble and quake.

My sister's call broke the spell again as I landed back on my proverbial feet.

"We're all set. Follow me!" announced Marissa, who didn't miss a beat in sending me a wink now that she was obviously all caught up. I'll have to remember to thank Mia later for saving me the repeat conversation and Spanish Inquisition.

"Shall we?" Kieran asked, as he placed his strong hand on the small of my back to lead me up the very tight, winding stone staircase to the Green Hall. The mere touch of him sent shivers down my spine as heat rose up throughout the rest of my body like ascending lava.

We were greeted by the dinner hosts—the Earl's butlers and ladies of the house dressed in medieval garb—with a glass of honey mead, the sweetness and strength of which made my head spin just a little bit more than the intoxication of Kieran's presence. I'll admit that it was so good, I snuck an extra mug of it when no one else was looking. Liquid courage was on my menu for the evening.

The beauty and intricacy of the Green Hall's carved walls left us feeling astounded. The colors of the fabric tapestries were richly gold with designs of reds, greens and purples—truly royal hues. The stained glass windows, expertly hand-designed furniture pieces and photos of ancestral stories brought the heritage of the castle to life.

As I closed my eyes to snap it into a photo in my mind, I could hear the pre-show music playing. I imagined I was back at some ancient royal gala and instinctively started to sway. Marissa was the one to catch me before I bumped into a stranger.

"You okay?" she wondered in amusement.

"I'm grand," I smiled back. "Oh Mar, isn't this place so amazing? I could have been a princess in this very castle in a past life. Could you imagine?"

"You being a princess? Yes. Finding you like this, all silly and carefree right now? No. But it is nice to see," she added with a rub to my back. "You deserve to be happy. Maybe your story is just beginning," she said with a blatant nod over to Kieran.

We both looked across the room, watching him laugh heartily as he greeted and interacted with strangers like he'd known them forever. His mere existence lit up the hall, not just for me, but seemingly for anyone who met him. Not unlike how Daddy could charm a room, I noted.

The air was bursting with joy and camaraderie unlike any event or party I'd ever been to. Kieran glanced over to catch us watching him and before I could blush, he raised his mug of honey mead with a wink and Cheshire cat smile before greeting another passerby with Gaelic glee.

It was finally time to gather around our table for the banquet to begin. The hall was set up with rows of long wooden tables and benches surrounded by the magnificent décor of feudal times, whisking me back to another time and space.

Kieran, clearly a gentleman, escorted all of us women to our bench seats before strategically taking his place beside me. We chitchatted with other out-of-towners who were seated at our table until the festivities were ready to start.

A group of young college-aged friends were backpacking through all of Ireland on their spring break.

A mother and daughter were celebrating a very special birthday. It was extraordinary to hear the stories of how others were brought here this very same night.

The Earl welcomed us with great fanfare while castle nobility sang and entertained us as we enjoyed our four-course feast (without silverware!). The tables were lit solely by candlelight for a truly antiquated, intimate feel.

It was a wonderful evening of mirth as we were serenaded by the famous Bunratty Castle Singers. I could feel the emotion rise to my eyes as I heard their angelic voices harmonize *Danny Boy* with such grace and beauty.

I felt Kieran reach for my hand under the table and give it a squeeze. I didn't even have to look at him to know he was equally moved by the musical synchronizations. I let my hand fall naturally into his as we enjoyed the show in between dinner and dessert.

From time to time, he would turn to me and we would talk about how he came to know Colleen, or I'd share some of my favorite adventures from the past few days as a tourist. Kieran seemed to get along rather well with my sisters, too, taking an interest in learning about Mia's children and enduring Marissa's gushing over her Hunt Museum experience and lifelong dream to become an artist.

If he only realized the true way to a girl's heart is through her sisters, then he'd know how sweet this moment was for me.

I didn't want the night to end. Not only because it was one of the most captivating dinner experiences I ever attended, but because of Kieran himself. A certain level of mystique was added to the evening with him being there beside me, secretly holding my hand out of view like we were forbidden lovers.

Yes—I was the countess and he was just some peasant man who stole my heart. I'd sneak out of my stone tower to meet him by the creek for a starlit night of passionate kisses. If I believed in past lives, I could imagine we did in fact live another story together.

Saddened that dessert was over, I wasn't ready for the fairy tale finale quite yet. I enjoyed playing pretend in my mind; a pastime I had long forgotten in exchange for cunning advertising and ruthless advancement.

"That would be a fierce performance! I enjoyed that I did, I did! Thank you for invitin' me. We best be off, though," Colleen said as she grabbed a complimentary coffee on our way out of the castle.

"So soon?" Mia asked on my behalf.

"Colleen here has her Sunday mass early in the morning. I promised to get her home for a decent night's rest," Kieran replied.

He turned to each one of us girls and kissed our hands. "Thank you for allowing me the pleasure of your company. I hope to see you again," he added, lingering a bit longer on my hand before the electricity turned back to darkness with his departure.

I wasn't going to get any sleep that night with all the thoughts and feelings rushing through my head— or Marissa's demands to fill her in completely. So, we extended our night by making the customary post-banquet stop at Durty Nelly's for a drink and sisterly conversation.

"Mia only filled me in enough to understand what was going on. Now dish it!"

Laughing, I told her the story until she was satisfied that she heard enough.

"So, you had no idea he was the caretaker when you met him? How sweet of him to try to see you again. I was watching him—he seems smitten with you." Mia observed in her cop-like way.

"Smitten? What are we, in grammar school?"

"I'm just saying that it's not in a way most guys look at girls these days. You could tell there was an attraction, but a respectful one. Not one of 'I want to get in her pants' but one of 'I'm intrigued by her.' Smitten seems to fit the bill.

"Plus, Colleen confirmed he was single and contrary to his looks, not a ladies man—except when it comes to charming old bitties, as she put it," she teased.

"I have to agree, Meg," Marissa chimed in. "He is quite the gentleman, though I'm pretty sure he wouldn't mind getting in your pants," she corrected. "I liked him very much."

"He does seem like a decent guy, doesn't he?"

"So, what's next?"

"I don't know. I mean, let's be real. We only have a little more than a week left here and then we're home and I'm back to the grind. I'm not sure I want to make a big deal of this. Maybe I should just accept this as one magical night and let it be."

"You could play it safe like you always do, sure," chided Marissa. "But what if you just let yourself take a chance for once. Who cares if you never see him after this trip?

"Why can't you just let down your guard and allow yourself to enjoy the romance of it all? Why do you have to see where this fits into your perfectly laid out future? You are here right now. The present moment is all you have—for once, just make the most of it."

"I know. I did just make a promise to myself to open up more and take new risks. I'm not going to chase him down, though. If our paths cross again, then I'll just take it from there."

"Oh, your paths will cross again. I know it," reassured Mia, like she had access to her own personal crystal ball.

The next morning, we found the road back to County Mayo to be relatively uneventful. The bus made a few stops along the way for some last-minute sightseeing, including to the pilgrimage sites of the Holy Mountain of Croagh Patrick and Our Lady of Knock—a famous shrine citing that Jesus, the Blessed Virgin Mary, Saint Joseph and Saint John the Evangelist once appeared there. I couldn't imagine ever having enough time to truly see all the wonders this country had to offer.

After what seemed like countless hours on a bus, we finally arrived back at the house shortly before dinner, grateful to settle into something more familiar and less over-populated. We were greeted by a handwritten note left by Kieran, welcoming us back and letting us know that his mum's colcannon fish pie need only be heated up for dinner tonight.

I was more than a little disappointed to have missed him and that there wasn't a personal touch to his note. Maybe it was just going to be that one charming evening after all.

We unpacked, ate the delicious dinner left for us and engaged in some light conversation about the highlights of our trip. We were pretty worn out from the travels but were looking forward to finally getting down to business.

Colleen was supposed to come over the next evening

to begin sharing some of the family stories and the purpose of us being here. I admit that I had forgotten all about it on our cyclone of a tourist tour.

I chose to sleep in the next morning, awakening to the sounds of Mia humming in the backyard garden below. I peeked out the window to see her happily pulling up the very few weeds that existed, smelling the flowers in her path and selecting a few for what I could only guess would be for tonight's table arrangement.

Marissa was further back towards the end of the yard in what appeared to be a flirtatious phone conversation, fingers twirling through her dark, loose tendrils. Curious. I wonder if that was her new little country lover or maybe Jay. Well, whoever it was, she was happy, and I was happy for her.

I strolled down the stairs to find a still-hot pot of coffee and kettle of water awaiting me. I chose a traditional black tea alongside a blueberry muffin with butter for breakfast. Not wanting to disturb my sisters or my solitude, I snuck outside to sit on the rocking chair, journal in hand, to get lost in some writing.

About an hour or so later, Marissa and Mia found me and shared the news that Colleen would not be able to meet up with us for another few days, as a house emergency came up that she had to tend to; something about her wretched plumbing.

Marissa wanted to take the opportunity to check out Clare Island for the next few days and booked a room at the Lighthouse, not knowing when we'd get the chance again to do more exploring.

"It is supposed to have the most spectacular sights! Since we've been so busy, I selected the spa relaxation package so that we could enjoy the tranquility of the scenery while we are there."

"I'm not up for another adventure just yet. Would you mind if I stayed behind?" The thought of traveling again was unsettling, even if it was a promise of a retreat. So much had happened in the past few weeks—so many emotions and revelations—that I craved some time alone to review it all.

"Of course," said Mia. "We are leaving this afternoon and will be back Tuesday night. If you change your mind, just let us know and you can always meet us there."

"That's a great idea. Maybe I will do that. I just need some time to myself. A lot to think about."

"We completely understand," Marissa agreed. "Oh, by the way, while I was walking this morning, a neighbor of ours—Mr. O'Dooly I think his name was—stopped to say hello. He was saying something about being a longtime friend of the family's and that he would be happy to check on the house while we were gone. Is it me or are people overly friendly and up in everyone's business over here?"

"Seems to be the way here," I chuckled. Every local was a town crier.

"Yeah well, just be careful, Meg," she cautioned. "He seemed harmless enough but was a little too interested in knowing why we're here and mentioned something about unusual activity in the neighborhood lately. Just stay safe."

"I will. I promise."

With a big bear hug from each, they were excitedly off to pack for their next escapade. I realized that meant I would be on my own for the first Sunday dinner in a very long time, but there were enough ingredients around for me to toss together something simple. I'd have to go back to the market tomorrow, but I had plenty to hold me over for today.

The thought of going there sent a whole garden of butterflies coursing through my stomach again. *Does Kieran go to the market every day? Would I run into him?*

Nonsense. I can't spend my entire time in sanctuary thinking about this man and wondering if fate would bring us together again. I actually had plans for something else while the girls were away—to dig into that attic.

I couldn't wait until Tuesday for Colleen—Mr. O'Dooly wasn't the only one curious about why we were here. *I need some answers now,* I said to myself as I looked up at the hauntingly beautiful portrait of my great-great-grandparents.

The house was unnervingly still with only the sounds of the rickety floors. It was a moment mystery novels thrived on, which made it all the more spine-chilling yet exciting at the same time. To calm my nerves, I pretended it was good old cousin Shane just checking in on me.

I found a large flashlight in one of the kitchen cupboards and armed myself with it as I ventured upstairs to the attic. It was just as I expected: dark, full of cobwebs and with treasures waiting to be discovered.

There were boxes of papers, a few old trinkets collecting dust here and there and some old, worn-out clothes. I wondered to myself why this stuff just wasn't thrown out or given away instead. I did happen upon a few exquisite dresses and hats that I imagined were quite the fashion back in the day.

Being a child at heart, I decided to try one of the dresses on. One was a royal blue, long-sleeved satin gown with intricate white lace overlaying the heart-shaped, form-fitting bodice. White sheer fabric flowed over the sleeves for an air of elegance. The bottom of the gown fell slightly past my ankles, trimmed with more lace in a whimsical floral pattern. Built-in ruffles underneath gave the dress volume and I felt like I was ready to go to a grand gala.

Needing to check my reflection and verify my newly imagined life as courtier, I carefully managed to get myself and this massive gown down the attic stairs and into my bedroom to take a peek in the full-length mirror. I decided to undo my ponytail so that my natural curls flowed over the shoulders of the dress freely.

I have to say, I couldn't help but admire how I looked in the medieval fabric. The coloring brought out the deepest hues in my eyes and its shape hugged my curves in all the right places.

Feeling noble, I twirled and curtsied, holding my hand out as if the imaginary prince standing there was waiting to kiss it and ask me to dance.

"Why, I would be honored to have this dance with you," I said out loud as I embraced an invisible lover in my arms and began to waltz. He twirled me around like the wind scooping up the fallen leaves.

I jumped when I saw Kieran standing in my bedroom doorway with an amused look on his face.

"You scared me half to death! What are you doing here?" Hand to my heart, I made my way over to the bed to catch my breath.

"I'm sorry, I didn't mean to frighten you. I didn't know anyone was here. Colleen told me you went off to Clare Island, so I'm after finishing up some work on the deck out back. I heard some noise inside and I thought I would come check it out. Seems like I interrupted a very important dance lesson," he said, suppressing a chortle.

"I was—um—I was up in the attic and found this dress and guess I just got caught up in the moment. I can't even begin to tell you how mortified I am." Still standing leaned up against the doorway, he traded his playfulness for a more serious, temperate tone.

"Don't be. You're not the only one to be found caught up in the moment. I thought ye an *aisling*."

"What's an ash-ling?"

"A vision. Megan, I didn't know if you were real until you started dancin'. You are the most beautiful woman I have ever seen."

He cautiously yet purposefully moved into the bedroom towards me. I was completely frozen as if trapped under ice. He stood just an inch away as he ran his fingers through my hair and caressed my cheek. He took my hand in his to lift me off the bed until I was only a breath away.

"I haven't been able to stop thinking about you and those eyes since that day at the market, *a ghrá*. You are unlike any woman I have ever met."

"I am?"

"Indeed." We locked gazes for a moment and the world stopped. He gently weaved his hand through the back of my hair to draw me closer as his lips touched mine. They were soft and full with the strength of a man but the restraint of a saint.

He lingered ever so lightly, letting me set the pace and intensity of our first kiss as he never once took those mesmerizing eyes off mine. With all the passion I never knew was inside of me, I drew him closer and gave him all of me in that single kiss.

I could feel the roughness of his unshaved scruff

against my skin, heightening the raw desire within. The smell of his pure masculine muskiness played with my senses, driving me to the brink of insanity. I pressed my body up against his, feeling the hardness of his chest muscles even through the layers of dress that separated our skin from touching. I ached for more.

Our lips parted, allowing our tongues to intertwine, seek, explore—setting off tiny explosions within my body. The heat rose between us, the natural voltage uniting more than just our lips. His hands, no longer tangled in my hair, took my face as he pulled away gently, pressing his lips to my nose and then tenderly to my forehead.

Why was he stopping? I didn't want it to ever end. As if he could read my mind, his broken, spent voice whispered, "Slow *a ghrá*, and let us savor this. 'It takes time to build castles.'"

I recognized the old Irish proverb from one of Granny's many teachings. How romantically clever of him. Pausing only to run his fingers through my hair and kiss my cheek once more, he started to turn away.

"Where are you going?" I asked, breathless.

"I think it best that you get yourself out of that dress before I do it for ya, lass. Meet me downstairs when you're ready. I want to show you something."

Obligingly, I grabbed a pair of jeans and a form-fitting green sweater from the top of the dresser drawer, fixed my hair and makeup and went down to the back door where Kieran was waiting for me. He took my hand and led me towards the back of the yard, where an enormous peach and fuchsia-colored rosebush was the spotlight of another well-groomed garden I hadn't yet noticed.

"I grew up hearing stories of the legendary love between your great-great grandparents, Cian and Alessia.

One of them was this here rose bush that they planted together. Now any true gardener can tell you a good solid rose bush can last only up to thirty-five or forty years, but not this one.

"Over a hundred years this one would be. Tended with love by the families that followed, stowing blessings upon the caregivers. It's become its own folklore around here."

"It's so beautiful. I've never seen roses that color before. They're so unique. Do you really think they are the original roses planted?"

"Ay. Love has a way of making things everlasting. Even if this bush here was actually replanted in secret several times over the years by new generations," he hinted, "it blooms nevertheless in the same sacred spot. Its magic has already taken hold."

"This entire country seems magical," I said wistfully. "How much do you know about my ancestors?"

"Not much. Just a bit here and there. From what I do know, there is rumored a scandal behind their love story— quite the holy show. I've always had a bit of curiosity about it, I have, but too much respect for the O'Sullivans and Collins' to be nosy about their business."

"Collins? Who's that?"

"Oh, that be Colleen's mother, Mary Collins, who married the old Banan O'Sullivan III. That's who she be living with now—her cousins on her mother's side. Ain't nary an O'Sullivan left, aside from Colleen and you all. Her dear brother Shane and his family tragically died in a boating accident off the shore of the Atlantic about ten years back. Nearly drowned herself in tears with grief. Which is why I reckon she was so tickled to learn of your existence."

"How horrible! To lose a brother and his whole family

like that? The more I hear, the more I realize I have yet to learn. That's why I was up in the attic before. I thought maybe I could find something to tell me a little bit more about our family history before Colleen has the chance to fill us all in.

"I feel so drawn here. I can't explain it Kieran, but I feel like I'm home, like I'm already part of the story."

"I find that enthralling. Say, would you like some help up there digging around? The deck can wait a bit more. If it's not an intrusion," he added considerately.

"I would love that, thank you. There were some boxes that were a bit on the heavy side for me. From what I can tell, you seem to have strong arms," I said, suggestively running my fingers down his shoulder all the way to his fingers.

I entwined them with mine as I smiled wickedly, feeling my confidence around him beginning to grow. "Let's go unravel a mystery."

Having someone who knew the ins and outs of the house was coming in fairly handy. Kieran scored another flashlight and an extension cord that let us light up the attic better with a small lamp. Amidst the dresses I had found earlier were more boxes—old kitchenware, some clothes bins and quite a few heavy loads of books.

I'm not sure what I was looking for—and even less sure of what I had gotten myself into. We spent a good part of an hour just looking through some of the box contents, sharing a few laughs about what we found but nothing that stood out as anything special.

That is, until I came across this one particularly small box marked "AO" in calligraphy. I opened it up to discover a bunch of old photos.

"Check this out."

"Ah, that be the same couple as photographed above the mantel. Quite the beautiful pair, for sure. You have his eyes, you know."

"I thought so, too. So, that's Cian and Alessia. And then here's Cian with another blonde man who looks just like him—do you know who that is?"

"I'd venture to say that's his older brother, Banan Junior—Colleen's granda."

"And here they are with a little girl—I think that might be my great-grandmother, Lena. Grandfather

Leigh's mother."

"I'd wager you're right."

"She's beautiful. She reminds me of Mia." I turned over the back to read the inscription and froze.

"What is it, *a ghrá*?"

"Nothing. Just that it says Mama, Papa and Diamond. That's what our grandfather used to call my mother before—before he took off and left her."

I couldn't control the bitterness that crept up inside me. All this heritage and we never knew about it. Heritage that our mother missed out on all these years.

"What do you suppose…" he asked as he pulled out a weathered leather-bound book from underneath the photos.

"It looks like a journal. Do you think it's okay to look at it?" There was something unsettling about finding someone's private thoughts in an attic—even if the ancestor died close to one hundred years ago.

"I don't see the harm in it." He handed it over to me so that I could open it, revealing a cover page with the name Alessia Bianchi originally written on it, but the Bianchi was crossed out and replaced by O'Sullivan. The first page was dated March 19, 1892. I couldn't help but stare at the perfection in her handwriting.

"You know what? Why don't we bring this box downstairs and get outta this manky attic? I'm famished— let's grab a bite before we dig into this, shall we?"

"That sounds like a good idea. I know we have some ingredients on hand to whip up an easy pot pie. I'm not much of a cook, but I can definitely handle that."

"Sounds grand. I'll grab a bottle of wine or two. Looks like we might be needing it tonight."

The evening was an unexpected pleasure. While I was

preparing dinner, Kieran had taken it upon himself to lay out a beautiful place setting with some white lace mats and napkins from one of the cupboards. Wine glasses were already filled with the souvenir honey mead we picked up from our Bunratty adventure.

Two single, tall-tiered candles sat upon silver holders giving the room a soft glow. In the background I could hear the sounds of Celtic instruments crooning their love songs. It made me wish my dinner itself had the same kind of amorous flare.

"My, aren't you talented at setting a mood," I teased. "No doubt this is how you get all your women to fall madly in love with you."

"To be honest, it's been a long time since I've wanted to go to such lengths to please a woman. I guess you be bringing out the best in me." There was that irresistible smile before he gently kissed me again on the lips. "Dinner smells delightful."

"I wouldn't be complimenting me just yet. Cooking is not my forte," I laughed.

"Well then, it be a good thing we have plenty of mead to wash it down with."

The conversation throughout dinner was light and spirited. He told me all about how he learned to play the piano and guitar as a young lad and how it inspired his love of music. I shared my stories about my father and all the places I wanted to visit, though I doubted anything could ever measure up to the beauty and awe of Ireland.

"It suits you just fine, ole Éire."

"I feel like I belong here. Work is constantly stressful, and my life back home is so hectic. But in Ireland, I am a completely different person. Calm and at peace. Does that sound crazy?"

"Yes."

"Really?"

"I'm just codding ya, lass. It's not crazy a'tall. I think whenever we're outside our environment, we feel a freedom to just be ourselves. It sounds like you've lost a bit of yourself back there. Well, I don't know *that* Megan, but I will say that I am completely beguiled by the Megan sitting in front of me."

"You're pretty charming yourself, *prionsa*."

"Prince, eh? Well, *mo banphrionsa*, shall we retire to the setting area to take a gander at that journal?"

Before I could respond, we heard a loud bang outside. Instinctively throwing the light on, Kieran made his way to the back door to investigate. Flashlight in hand, he did a quick scan of the yard, lingering in the bushes to make sure nothing was hiding there. Satisfied that there was nothing to see, he protectively double locked the door and checked the front to make sure we were nice and secure.

"Was prolly just a critter trying to get into your trash. 'Tis a bit cold around these parts still and they'd be looking for something to eat. Here, let me set the fire and get us all warmed up. There's a blanket in that drawer if you can grab it and I could do with a bit more drink, if you don't mind."

Within minutes, he had the fire blazing and we settled down on the sofa with our glasses of honey mead and the journal. Not that we needed the warmth or the excuse for closeness, but the heavy wool blanket bound us tightly together. It felt so natural to nestle into the grooves of his chest as he brought his strong, protective arm around me and held me close.

How could it be that I already felt such a familiarity with a man I literally met a week ago?

We read the first few pages together and I suddenly realized how helpful it was to have my own personal translator. Fortunately, Kieran already knew the Italian language well; much better than the few courses I took in college. Although I could get the gist of what Alessia was writing, some of the references and slang she used were beyond my American comprehension.

After reading a couple of her initial entries, I lost hope in this being the juicy tell-all I had envisioned.

No, it was simply some young girl's daily dream-doodling about her chats with girlfriends, an unrequited crush who ignored her and an annoyance over a teacher's dismissal of her academic abilities. What was crystal clear was her fiery spirit and love of life, however.

Page after page we read on, hoping to find something, anything that might give me insight into the mystery of why we were here; what this secret heritage was really all about. Before I knew it, I sensed myself being carried up the stairs and placed into my bed.

"What—what are you doing?" I asked groggily.

"You're completely shattered, *a ghrá*. You fell asleep mid-sentence. Why don't you get some shut eye and I'll check on you in the mornin'? I'll lock up and leave a light on downstairs."

Too tired to fight, I allowed him to cover me with a warm blanket and darken the shades in my bedroom. He set the journal—earmarked on the last page we read—on the dresser before coming back over to the bed.

Bending over to caress the stray piece of hair from my face and place a gentle kiss on my forehead, I heard him whisper gently in Gaelic what must have been the equivalent of good night, as I drifted off into a peaceful slumber.

Was it all just a dream? I woke up feeling dazed, but when I saw myself still in the clothes from the day before under the blanket, I knew that the evening with Kieran was as real as the sunlight beaming in through the window.

Shivers and goosebumps ran down my body as I noted that the warmth that was once Kieran was no longer surrounding me. The sensation of hope traveled back into my heart when I saw a text message from him waiting on my phone.

Good morning, a ghrá. Hope you slept well. Need to grab some messages for Mum this morning. See you at noon? Your Kieran.

My Kieran. I smiled at the thought of that. Wait— what am I doing? I can't get caught up in all this mushy stuff after one day. I can enjoy my time with him, indulge in some kisses and attraction, but pretending it can be anything other than a brief interlude is insane. Still, I couldn't resist sending an equally saccharin message back.

Good morning, prionsa. I'm heading to the market myself this morning. Noon is perfect. Until then, Your Megan.

With that all settled, I jumped into the shower and decided on a bright floral dress and white sweater. I let my hair hang down to dry naturally into waves, knowing the fresh air would do a better job than a blow dryer would (especially since I forgot the electrical converter to plug it into). Grabbing my bags and the basket I forgot to return last week, I set out for the market on an unusually warm day—possibly the warmest we'd had since arriving.

Enjoying the glorious morning, I waved to each local as I passed them by. All I could think of was meeting up with Kieran again and reading more of my great-great-grandmother's journal. I was so lost in the tunnels of my mind that I hadn't noticed the shadow behind me.

I thought maybe I was being followed, but as I turned around, I only saw the friendly neighbors I had just greeted. I cautiously continued on my way, glancing back occasionally to check, but finding nothing. Still, I just couldn't shake the eerie feeling.

You watch way too many suspense films, Meg.

I made it in and out of the market without incident this time. And since I had some extra time to spare, I decided to pop into a few of the shops to do some souvenir shopping. I came upon a traditional wool store and settled on matching pink sweaters for Mom and Granny. I also found some matching eggshell-colored woolen glove and scarf sets that my nieces and nephew might actually not be embarrassed to wear—teens were so hard to buy for.

I also stopped by a little jewelry store and picked up three matching Celtic bracelets to commemorate our sister trip to Ireland and purchased an extra trinity pendant for myself. There were some pretty earrings I found for my nieces and engraved money clips I thought Stephen and Kevin might like. Pleased with my shopping experience, I made my way back home.

Home. Who would have thought some old little house in the Middle of Nowhere, Ireland would feel like home.

Smiling at the thought, I grabbed Alessia's journal and settled into the side garden.

It was more of the same boring teenage diatribe for a while. Here and there, I found juicy nuggets relating to her relationship with her family (thank goodness for Google's online translation assistance), including how strict her father was about the men she was allowed to date—"no one outside of her kind." I could see where that was headed. Finally, a hint into this alleged scandal.

She also talked about her lack of respect for her mother's constant fear and siding with her father over everything, from manners to societal expectations. And how her parents were so much easier on her two younger sisters, putting more pressure on Alessia to marry well and bear heirs as the eldest since there were no sons to continue the family business.

I deciphered that she wasn't all that fond of her younger sister, Dominica, who broke every rule known to man and got away with it. To paraphrase: a party girl who loved her men but still presented herself to elders as the perfect noble lady that parents could be proud of. I could hear the resentment in Alessia's voice as she spoke about the unfairness of it all.

She did seem to speak affectionately of her meek little sister, Concetta. At least there seemed to be someone in the poor girl's corner.

The morning passed quickly, and right on time, my sexy Irishman strode up to the side of the house to greet me with a kiss and a bouquet of gorgeous pale pink and purple heath spotted-orchids, native to County Mayo.

"They're beautiful, thank you. I'm not sure I am going to survive all this spoiling."

"'How can a woman be expected to be happy with a

man who insists on treating her as if she were a perfectly normal human being?'"

"Oscar Wilde. Well done," I said, acknowledging his poetic reference. "'The very essence of romance is uncertainty,'" I countered with another Wilde quote. He lifted his eyebrows in acceptance of my matching wit.

"Ay, is that a challenge? I shall mind myself to not become predictable then."

With those words, he grabbed me into a heated embrace, not waiting for my permission before his lips and tongue were exploring mine in rushed desire. His right hand holding my face locked against his as his left started to smoothly explore my back, inching lower towards my waist so that he could pull the full of my body against his.

For a moment, we were simply lost in this passionate hold that paused the orbiting of the universe—until I had to pull away, realizing that we were outside for any passerby to see.

"What's wrong, *a ghrá*?"

"Nothing. Just that there are neighbors all around and—"

"This be Ireland, lass. Nobody minds witnessing grand expressions of fondness, especially when the lovers are in one's own garden. Gives 'em something new to gossip about anyways," he proposed.

"Still I—" I broke off, embarrassed, frazzled. I didn't want the kiss to end. But if I didn't end it, I would have given in to the deep hunger I felt right there on the spot.

Pull it together, Megan. You're treading in dangerous territory.

Sensing my hesitation, Kieran respectfully pulled back.

"I have an idea. Why don't you grab a sweater and

we can take a walk down to the creek? Get some fresh air. Then you can tell me all about what you've been reading in that there journal. I brought a few sandwiches and whatnot with me and we can have lunch at the park if you're hungry."

"That sounds really nice. I saw a wicker basket in one of the closets. I'll grab that and a blanket for the ground. If you could grab some wine and glasses and maybe a few snacks from the kitchen, we can have ourselves a picnic."

"A bit of a romantic yourself, are you now?" I was perilously worshipping that smile of his—the perfect balance of boyish grin and manly warmth. He didn't need words when his mouth expressed it all. Now I was even more grateful for choosing to stay behind while my sisters went off on their spa retreat.

Since the creek was further down past the shops and over the bridge, I enjoyed the new scenery as we explored more of the village. Along the way, I noticed a small brick church with stained glass windows—the kind that looked like it could have doubled as a schoolhouse back in the day. I adored the antique character of this town.

There was another stone structure nearby that was in complete ruins, which Kieran explained was an ancient wedding altar—an extension of the church. Those who were wed in that very spot were said to be supernaturally blessed in their unions by the presence of goddesses, fruitful in their procreation of children and in their lifelong trades.

Legend had it that a forbidden couple secretly exchanged vows there, but when the young woman's betrothed found out about it, he brought a small army of friends and weapons to destroy the altar the next day, setting a curse upon the lovers.

Now it was reduced to rubble and overgrown weeds, but I imagined if someone really wanted to, they could properly restore it to its original splendor. Yet still, even in ruins, it was not an eyesore but an intriguing bit of history that hid a whimsy of enchantment that felt an awful lot like the energy surrounding the Witch Stone.

Along the way, I filled Kieran in on the passages I had read in the journal and the conclusions I formed about Alessia and her family. He agreed that it sounded spot on, recalling that he had heard her union with Cian was not one her father approved of and that she had left her family to live here in Ireland, where the folks were a bit more accepting.

We finally came across the little creek, its clear water trembling over natural gray, mossy rocks with a few strategically placed man-made stepping stones. Before it lay an open, lush green meadow of land and a small forest of pine trees—the kind Bambi would've surely frolicked in.

We set out the blanket upon the grass; the morning dew dried up by the daycs sun. Kieran poured some of the leftover honey mead from last night into our glasses while I set out the spread of food. We toasted to a beautiful day, to the company and to the mysterious journey we were on. I inhaled the truth of where we were.

"So, this is truly where I came from. My ancestors not only lived in that very house, but as children, they must have come down to this stream to play. If I close my eyes, I can see Alessia washing out some knickers as Lena takes off her socks and shoes to go wading and splashing right here. Cian's in the background, sitting on the ground with a pipe enjoying the sight of it all."

"You have quite the imagination there, Miss Megan.

Ever put it to good use?"

"As a young girl, I loved to write stories. Then as I grew older and realized there wasn't much stability to be had in such a fly-by-night field, I turned to advertising. I was still able to write and create, but in a different way. I turned out to be very good at it—being able to take a client's vision and turn it into their reality."

"But what about your visions, *a ghrá*? Sure it's grand to bring their dreams to life, but how do you express yours?"

"I was—*am*—fine with it. I infuse my ideas into theirs. It's natural for me and I've gained a lot of respect and credibility as an executive because of my work. Having that control, prestige and stability was enough for me, so I put my writing on the back burner.

"I'm my own woman because of it, Kieran. A woman I am proud of, who can fend for herself and thrive in a man's world. Sometimes, childhood dreams have no place there."

"Creation is like a heartbeat. Without it, you slowly die until the heart stops beating completely."

"Whose quote is that?"

"Mine."

Overlooking the water rushing down, my tears started matching pace with the realization that he was right. All these years, I'd been gradually fading away until I no longer recognized my reflection. When those middle school boys grabbed at my matured breasts and the school did nothing about it, my spirit hardened and it changed the softness of my baby face.

When Scotty shattered my heart, I closed the door to love and affection, further aging my soul and darkening the sparkle of my eyes. Fighting man after man on my way up the corporate ladder, weathering sexist advances and countless hours seeking validation, I continued to erode inside and forget the young girl who used to dream up a much more positive expectation from life.

Alas, life was not a fairy tale I could write away.

Daddy dying was the nail in my coffin; no longer would he be there to argue with me in an attempt to help me see and release the light of my soul that I was burying away. Every year, I burrowed another foot under the ground. He died before he could save me. I now understood the angst I'd see in his eyes when he'd look at me; like he had failed me.

But he didn't. He never could. I was the one who failed myself.

I felt Kieran come up behind me and gently wrap his arms around me, kissing the back of my head before laying his chin on my shoulder.

"When I look at you, I see so much passion inside. I'm not just talkin' about your physical fire that's hard for me to resist, mind you. I see the fiery spirit of a woman who indeed is independent and strong but is also witty and playful and yearnin' to tell a story of her own making.

"Your mind is not limited to executing the dreams of others, *a ghrá*. You can still run with the wolves of men and be the inspired woman you are inside. I can feel your true essence, Megan, and it moves me to share mine."

"I want to write again," I whispered, finally admitting what was truly burning in my heart. "I do feel alive when I let it out on paper. It feels right." I turned to look at him, feeling the fear bubble up inside as I considered how following my heart would turn my whole world upside down.

"But how can I just throw away an empire I helped

to build? How can I turn my back on everything I have worked so hard for and risk losing everything?"

"No one is saying you have to give up your job. You can still kick arse in advertising and be that woman. But maybe cut back on the hours you spend making others happy and invest them into your own passions instead. You don't have to make that choice—you just need to follow what calls to your soul."

"That's the problem. I don't know where my heart begins and where my head ends. I can't figure it all out right now and it scares me. I had a plan, Kieran. That empire was my plan.

"But the more time I spend here—the more time I spend with you—it feels empty. But it's all I know. Work is all I have been able to trust in and rely on, except for my family of course. I'm terrified of not seeing how the future unfolds. I used to be so certain and now, I can't even see past tomorrow."

"All we have is this moment, today. It's all we ever have. But that's the beauty of following creation. It brings us the future. We don't have to design the unknown. That's God's work. Our job is to simply live."

"That's an awfully tall order for a control freak," I admitted nervously.

"Then let someone else take the lead for a change," he responded as he leaned in to kiss me. The slow graze of his lips burned into a more zealous yearning to dive in deeper. He laid me back onto the blanket smoothly, moving his kisses from my lips to my neck and then to that sweet spot right under my ear. With a tug of my lobe, my body responded with an aching desire for more.

He moved to my side and still lingering around my neck with his hot breath and mischievous bites, I could feel his warm, slightly rough hands move down, under and into the bodice of my dress to cup my breast and tease my nipple ever so slightly. My back arched in pleasure, willing him to continue his exploration of my body.

I moaned at his touch, reaching my hand under his shirt to feel the power of his own tight, hot chest, prompting him to sit up and remove it completely. The way the sunlight circled around him and the fervent gleam in his eyes as he looked at me—only me—made him the most exquisite man I had ever seen. Yes, he was definitely a Celtic God reincarnated on earth.

We locked gazes for only a moment before his mouth was back on mine and the weight of his body consumed me. I couldn't resist running my hands up and down his muscled back, feeling him shudder as I teased with some light scratching of my fingernails.

He pulled up and off me slowly, running his hands through his hair as he blew out a hurricane of hot air.

"I think it best we take this somewhere more private, lass. And swiftly, because with the way those incredible blues are shining up at me, I just might hafta take you right here and public be damned."

Agreeing, I promptly sat up and gathered everything together in the basket as he pulled his shirt back on. I fussed to throw my hair back into a respectable ponytail and straightened my dress, though anyone looking at us could tell that we were recently engaged in more than just conversation. Hand in hand, we walked back in contented silence towards the house, as if words would shatter the beauty of the moment.

10

I reached for my key as we neared the door, only to find that it was wide open.

Bizarre, I could have sworn it was locked before we left, I thought to myself.

Oh well, maybe Mia and Marissa came back a day earlier than expected. Or maybe Colleen was able to stop by sooner after all. Frustrated at the idea of entertaining anyone other than Kieran, I pushed my way into the house with him behind me as I called out their names.

But we didn't find anyone there—what we walked into was a completely trashed house. Papers, blankets, pillows, books and artifacts were all over the floor. Not completely broken; more like tossed aside. Drawers and pantries were opened and emptied.

I froze in place—who would do such a thing?

Kieran immediately called the Westport Garda, bringing me back out to the sidewalk in front of the house in case the perpetrator was still inside. Luckily, the Irish police were on site within ten minutes to check the place out, though we didn't see any sign of someone moving about the house or leaving since we had returned. Everything remained still.

"What a haymes! Do you know who's wantin' to be doing this to you, or what they were looking for?"

"No, no idea," I whispered as I answered a bunch

of routine questions. After they did an initial clearing of the house to make sure no one was there and dusted for evidence, they let us back in to see if I noticed if anything was missing. I told them it was hard to tell, since my sisters and I were only guests, but looking in our rooms, it appeared as if nothing of value was taken.

Strange—why didn't they take any of the jewelry we brought from home or any of the clearly valuable artwork that was placed throughout? As far as I could tell, nothing was missing; just ruffled.

I felt violated. It wasn't my home, but I was staying in it, so it was a personal betrayal. Did they know I wasn't there? What if I *was* inside? What if they were armed and I was in the wrong place at the wrong time? And then I remembered back to earlier this morning, when I felt as if I was being followed.

"You never mentioned you were being followed!" Kieran accused as he ran his hand in frustration through his hair. "Why didn't you tell me? Feck."

"I'm sorry, I just didn't think anything of it. I thought it was my imagination. I kept looking back and didn't see anyone, so I thought it was just a critter again."

"Ah, my money's on that not bein' a critter last night, neither."

"Marissa did warn me about a Mr. O'Dooly who was overly interested."

"That old coot? He's an odd one for sure, but harmless. I'll check it out, though. Wait right here with Commissioner Brady. I have a few calls to make."

Nodding my head, I sank down into the living room armchair. Another neighbor from down the street stuck her head in to find out what the commotion was all about and knowing her well, Commissioner Brady allowed her inside to sit with me.

"Hi dear. I'm Ellie Walsh from just a few doors down. I seen you and your sisters here with Colleen. She filled me in on your visit before you came. Here, I brought you a cuppa tea," she said sweetly as she handed me an insulated mug of chamomile and honey.

A plump old woman, no doubt close in age and best buddies with Colleen, she had a full head of wavy white hair and a heavily wrinkled face that couldn't hide her soft, green eyes of kindness.

"Thank you," I managed. "I don't know who could do such a thing."

"Don't you be worrying about that. Our Garda boys here are as good as they come. They're after catching that dosser, they are. It's a small town and someone musta seen somethin' around here. We see everything," she winked with a knowing smile that made me turn red.

"Nah, don't you be needin' to turn scarlet about that, neither. Our Kieran is a fine thing, he is indeed, a good honest fella. With that face he could be havin' lots o' mots but his mum raised him fine and proper to be a gentleman. I reckon he is sweet on you the way he is being all protective."

"He's a very good man," I agreed. "I wonder where he went, though?"

On cue, he came in through the back door and headed straight for me. "Good day, Mrs. Walsh. Thank you for looking out for my Megan."

"Ah 'twas not a thing. I best be going now but glad you're all right. I am down in the light yellow house now if you need anythin' a'tall."

"Thank you again for the tea. It was lovely to meet you." And it was. Her presence was soothing, like her tea.

Like Granny's tea. It made me really miss home and my sisters.

"I have to call Mia and Marissa and tell them what happened."

"Wait a minute, lass. I called Colleen and we agreed to let your sisters be for the day. It would only cause more chaos to bring them home right now. I've spoken with the Garda and after they help us clean up the place, they'll be leaving an armed guard here for the time being."

"An armed guard? Am I in danger?"

"I don't know, *a ghrá*. This kind of thing doesn't happen often 'round here. We'll be takin' every precaution we can. And I won't have any arguing about it, but I'll be stayin' here with you until your sisters return. I won't get a wink of sleep unless I know for myself that you're all right."

"Okay." Everything was happening way too fast; the room started to spin like a tilt-a-whirl at an amusement park. I felt Kieran pick me up and mutter something to the Garda about taking me up for a rest. This was becoming a habit it seemed, him carrying me lifeless to bed.

When I woke up, the house was tranquil, and the sky had darkened. Everyone must have left. That is, everyone except Kieran, who was resting comfortably in the lounge chair beside my bed thumbing through Alessia's journal.

"Good evening, sleepyhead. How was your rest?"

"Good. What time is it?"

"Half past seven. You've been asleep for quite a while."

"Have you been sitting there this whole time?"

"I have. You're just as beautiful asleep as you are

awake, ya know. Like an angel." I blushed at the thought of him watching me, and at the thought of him staying by my side for the next 24 hours.

"How's the house?"

"Most of it is cleaned up. It's just this room and a small part of the setting area that we didn't get to yet, but we can tackle that tomorrow. Hungry?"

"Starving. I picked up some food today. Or we can just reheat some leftover pot pie."

"I promised the boys to thank them for their help today with a pint. Let's get you out of this house for a spell. I know a great place," he winked as if he knew a secret I didn't.

"Sure. Let me just freshen up and I'll meet you downstairs."

The house was exactly as he said—you wouldn't have known that only a few short hours ago, it was completely in shambles. Still, I could feel the anxiety rise as I walked through the living room and spotted an officer standing guard outside of the back door. I was instantly relieved by the thought of getting out of this place, though I worried about what would happen again when we left.

"Billy and Horace have this place under tight watch," he said, reading my mind. "Not to mention your do-good neighbors who are on alert. There ain't nobody who'd get at it again. You're safe with us."

I smiled meekly up at him, letting him lead me to his truck. Before opening the door, he took me tightly into his arms and kissed me tenderly. "You look mighty pretty, by the way."

Finally noticing him through the fog of my thoughts, I saw he changed his clothes from earlier and had his hair slicked back. He donned a black leather jacket and ripped black jeans with matching work boots, looking sexy as hell.

The smell of his cologne wafted through my nose, setting off little twinges of longing throughout my body. Was it even possible for him to look more gorgeous in the moonlight than in the sun?

"You clean up well yourself, handsome. Where are we going?"

"To my favorite little pub. Great food, great music and I know the owner pretty well. Fantastic guy," he said, grinning mischievously.

A few moments later, we arrived at a place called Gov's and I looked at him curiously. He only smirked as he opened my car door, took my hand and escorted me into the loud, rowdy pub. Celtic rock music was blaring from the band on stage, laughter filled the air and you could smell the Guinness in pints all around.

"It's quite busy for a Monday night," I yelled over the din of the crowd.

"At Gov's, every night is Saturday night," he beamed.

Recognized by a table of officers and other guests, a raucous cheer and raising of glasses announced Kieran's arrival. We went over to greet his fans, introducing me as "his" Megan, the American lass who stole his heart. It earned him some teasing, but they were all so goodhearted in nature.

"Quite the place your Kieran has, doesn't he?" said a short, rotund little rascal affectionately known as Tuggs.

"Wait—this is *his* place?"

"It is! I reckon, who did you think Gov's belonged to?" The lightbulb went on. Of course. Short for MacGovern. I made my way over to a smaller table of guests where Kieran was now obviously playing host to. After a quick introduction, he excused us to a more quiet space in the room—though anywhere you went had you yelling just to be heard.

"Why didn't you tell me you owned a pub?"

He boyishly shrugged his shoulders. "It just never came up. It was me da's, and when he passed away ten years ago, it was his wish for me to carry it on. I have, with the help of a few partners. But they know better about the running of the business, for certain. Me, I'm in it for the music and the people. You'll have to excuse me for a moment though, because I'm gettin' the eye that I'm late."

"Late? For what?" I tried to ask as he kissed my cheek and carried himself off towards the front of the pub.

I looked around for a few minutes trying to find him. Good old Tuggs passed by and noticed I was without a pint, so he graciously bought me one and asked me to join him and his buddies at their table at the front of the room.

"Do you know where Kieran went? I can't seem to find him."

"Look up, lass. He be right there on the stage." And so he was, standing behind an electronic keyboard. Within moments, the band started playing and the energy level of the room went through the roof.

The lead singer had a sultry, sexy voice that crooned rock lyrics, while the two guitarists, drummer and Kieran on keyboard all took turns with their musical solos. It was hard not to dance and get into the feeling of the music, song after song.

I would catch glimpses of Kieran looking over at me while he performed, but it was when he looked away and released himself to his music that I knew exactly what he meant when he said he could see my essence. That was pure Kieran. Musical, lyrical, free.

Was I absolutely, completely falling in love with this man I just met, against my better judgment? Or was I just getting wrapped up in all this elated giddiness? Then I remembered my promise to myself to just let go and be in the moment.

When the set ended, he made his way through the crowd to come find me. Drenched with sweat, he exuded pure, raw sexiness. I threw my arms around his neck and jumped up to circle my legs around his waist, planting a hot smacking kiss on his lips.

"That was amazingly hot!" I exclaimed, hearing the room break out in applause over my amorous greeting. I turned all colors of crimson as I jumped down onto the floor. Kieran simply laughed and raised his fist up in the air in triumph.

He led me to a small table in the corner of the room while a waitress, as if trained in the art of serving Kieran, instantly brought over two pints, two burgers and a bucket of fries to our table.

"Thanks, Lily!"

"You betcha, boss!" She turned to me with a wink. "You know, this one's a keeper. If I weren't already madly in love with me own fella, I'd be tryin' to steal this man's heart away. But from the looks of it, there ain't no other girl in the world the way he be lookin' at you, so it'd be a fool's wish."

Kieran shot her a glare of warning. "Just musing, that's all," she muttered as she went to her next table.

He was right about Gov's—the food was delicious, as was the music and the ambiance. It was definitely what I needed to feel better after today. Just being around all the elation was enough to lift the poorest of spirits up.

"How about getting out of here?"

"But don't you need to stay and take care of business or play again?"

"Beauty of being the boss. I call the shots and I call it a night off with my girl. Besides, my crew has it all under control. Best a man could ever ask for."

Returning to the house brought reality all back. In my mind, I knew we were well guarded, and it did make me feel better to know that Kieran was staying with me, too, but I just couldn't put away the disconcerting feeling. I sat down among the disheveled mess that still waited for us in the setting room, trying to understand why this all happened. What was this person looking for?

"Here, *a ghrá*. Have some of this." He handed me a shot of whiskey, which I took willingly, as he sat down beside me.

"I just don't understand. Who would want to do this?"

"I don't have an answer for ya. I've been trying to wrap my head around it myself." I let my body fall back into his arms as we silently watched the fireplace flames flicker. I caught the chill of the poorly ventilated house and shuddered.

I felt him move my hair slightly so that he could press his warm lips to my neck and squeeze me closer. The chills came rushing back, but they were chills of excitement. His lips and hands traveled together, touching, feeling, exploring.

I turned my head and moved my body so that I could take his full lips on mine. I could taste the faint whiskey mixed with his own exotic flavor that I'd come to crave. The tenderness subsided and passion soared through our bodies, daring us to give more of ourselves than we ever had before.

He lifted me from the couch and carried me up the stairs. He stopped as he reached my bedroom door and just smiled.

"What's the matter?" I asked, perplexed.

"Nothing a'tall. It's just nice to have you conscious as I carry you to your bed for a change."

We laughed as he set me down and took a step back to close the door. He just stood there, barely a shadow in the darkened room. He grabbed a lighter from the dresser and lit the lilac candles that were part of the bedroom décor.

Moving back towards me, he never took his eyes off mine for a second, not even as he expertly unbuttoned my blouse and removed it. Pleasantly surprised to find a delicate pink camisole instead of a bra, he let his fingers trace the contours of my breasts under the lace as his teeth erotically pulled the straps down off my shoulders.

His lips nuzzled back into the groove of my neck, finding those subtle places that drove me to the brink of ecstasy. His hands disposed of the camisole, returning just as swiftly to feel the softness of my breasts and the tightening of my nipples exposed in the cool air.

I returned the favor by pulling his shirt off over his head, placing my hands on his bare chest and then around to his back. It was my turn to explore the pleasure spots of his neck and shoulders, feeling more aroused by his manly moans.

Our lips found their way back together as our hands began unbuttoning each other's pants. We both glided out of our remaining clothes, our two naked bodies being all that remained in the moonlight, aching to be joined as one.

Kieran tenderly led me to the bed, but I decided to maneuver his body under mine instead. I wanted to savor every part of this man, this beautiful man, who had not only revived my sexual passion but also my heart and soul.

I could feel him wanting to fight me, but I simply shook my head and let my persuasive eyes beg him to let me have my way. He obliged, after first pulling me down by my hair in a long, hard kiss. The pure touch of our bare bodies made my insides pulse, but I didn't want to rush this moment. I was so used to hard and fast goodbyes that I wanted to savor this relatively new experience.

I pulled my lips away from his and began my journey. I started at the base of his neck, a spot I found to be one of his weaknesses. My lips and hands headed south, licking, biting and kissing my way down his hairless, toned chest. I could feel his back arch slightly, which only deepened my desire to please him.

As I lingered my tongue around his pecs, I allowed my hand to wander down to wrap around his hardness. Stroking lightly, groans escaped and I could feel his need to rebel against my control and turn me over. I ignored his pleas, pushing aside his hands as I let my mouth travel further to where it yearned to go, enjoying every taste of his sinfully delicious body.

Unable to wait anymore, he overturned me so that the weight of his entire body pinned me down like a wrestler. Using a single hand to raise my arms above my head and restrain them, he grinned wickedly as he frustratingly did nothing but look at me for a while. "My turn."

He began by sensually taking one of my fingers into his mouth and kissed his way down my arm, and back to my neck and ears. It didn't take long for him to find my nipples waiting for his mouth to consume them and raise them into even more hardened mountainous peaks. Rushes of electric waves raced through me as he nipped them, escalating the sensations throughout my entire body.

With his mouth content where it was, his hand traveled down to discover the rainforest of wetness that awaited him. His mere touch triggered fireworks. He found my throbbing clit and began his expert massage, heightening all of my senses to madness.

Just when I thought I couldn't take any more, he released his hold with a look of warning that I was not to move and I obeyed. I could feel his tongue travel over my stomach and downward, finding me again and bringing me to the edge of orgasm. I felt the explosive rush take over, the pureness of ecstasy exposed—but he wasn't done.

He expertly glided inside of me, his hardness a perfect fit. Grabbing onto his back and winding my legs around him, I took him in deeper. With each thrust, we moved in sync like the harmonies of his rock band. I could feel the build rising again, wanting more, yet forbidding its end.

Gentle at first, the thirst quickened to uncontrollable desire until our mutual release left us both spent and completely satisfied. I could feel the weight of his body relax onto mine, not yet ready to pull out and disconnect us from the moment.

When he did, he rolled to the side to take me into his arms and plant a sacred kiss on my forehead.

"I know we've only just met, but I need you to know that I've never felt for another woman what I feel for you. I don't know what you're doin' to me lass, but you're suddenly stealing all of me." He intertwined his fingers with mine and moved in closer so that I could feel his breath on my neck.

"I'm not sure I can quite find the words to describe how I feel right now either."

"Then I guess I will just have to settle for you showing me," he suggested, as he kissed me into an endless night of lovemaking.

11

Waking up in the morning beside Kieran felt right; like he belonged there. Our naked bodies curved into each other like the perfect puzzle pieces. I carefully pulled free of his grip, noticing how one of his hands found a comfortable spot cupping my breast as he slept. It pained me to remove myself from him in any way, but I was hungry from a long, active night and wanted to surprise him with breakfast.

I managed to leave the bed without disturbing him, and as I looked back over at him, I understood what he meant when he said I was beautiful when I slept. He was a magnificent vision at rest, his dark hair a tousled mess; his face nestled sideways into the pillow.

Ah, we have a snorer here, I chuckled quietly to myself as I heard the muffled sound escape. At least it's not too bad—I hope. *Could be a deal breaker,* I thought humorously.

Grabbing a robe out of the closet, I made my way down the stairs to see what I could rustle up. I settled on making some scrambled eggs loaded with cheese, bacon and tomatoes atop rye toast. Fast and easy. As generous as I felt in making breakfast, I wasn't in the mood to make a big spread.

I was tired—believe it or not—of daily scones and endless carbs, so I had picked up some fresh berries for a mixed fruit salad.

Standing there over the stove, I realized that I had no idea if he was a coffee or tea person or if he was even a morning or night person. There was so much yet to discover about him.

I decided on making a large fresh pot of coffee anyway and added more ingredients to the pan to offer breakfast to the two officers standing guard outside. They were both grateful for the sustenance, as they were growing weary waiting for the shift change. Apparently, there was one already during the night—every eight hours—and no one had recorded any activity or disturbances, which made me feel more at ease.

Turning back to work in my little kitchen, I started washing and preparing the fresh blueberries, strawberries and raspberries for my fruit bowl. I remembered a recipe from a friend that called for adding some slivered almonds, coconut flakes and a touch of honey, so I thought I'd experiment a little like Mia does—and hope for the best. As I began mixing it all together, I sensed my lover coming up behind me.

"Well, what do we have here?"

"I made you a hearty American-style breakfast. Hope you're hungry!"

"Ravenous," he said, as he bit the back of my neck. "But I could use a meal as well."

He didn't care that I was busy, turning me around to face him so he could kiss me good morning. I lost track of what I was doing, instantly responding to his seductive invitation for a different kind of breakfast. We were both startled enough to pull apart when I dropped a spoon on the floor, bringing me back to my task at hand.

"Behave yourself, Gov," I warned. "Let me finish this

or we'll die of starvation."

"It'd be a grand way to go," he smirked.

"Still. Oh, what do you drink in the morning? I wasn't sure if you liked coffee, tea, juice?"

"Coffee, black. Usually just a single mug of it to get me goin' after a long night. Sometimes two." Walking over to the back door, he waved at the guard, noticing he got a head start on the chef's breakfast. "What's the story?"

"Duke said that everything went smoothly and that nothing happened. It was a boring night."

"Maybe for them," he teased. "I'm glad. Hopefully the eejit will keep his or her distance from here."

"I hope so, too. But I feel pretty safe right now."

With breakfast practically finished, I made my way over to the table to set it. I started humming one of the band's rock tunes that got stuck in my head from last night. It was more of a ballad and something about it just tugged at my soul.

"Ah, *Dream Rose*. You liked that song, did ya?"

"I did. It was hauntingly beautiful, with such heart."

"Out of the shadows and into the light
Dream Rose, she appeared
No longer a vision at night
Just a touch away, I feared
That I may sleep to watch her disappear

My heart and my life
How could I ever carry on
Without my sweet Dream Rose
Forever here by my side"

Stunned, I could only listen in awe as his pure sultry tone sang the words to the music that played repeatedly in my mind.

"I had no idea you could sing. You have an incredible voice. Is it one of the covers your band plays?"

"No. An original."

"Wow. Your band wrote it? Whoever knows how to put words and music together sure knows what he or she is doing."

"It was me. I wrote it the night I came home from the Bunratty banquet," he said with a rare vulnerability that touched me. "I wrote it about you. You're my own Dream Rose, like one from the magical bush out yonder. Life hasn't been the same since you ran over my foot."

I was speechless. No one had ever written a song about me, let alone sang it to me. I could only respond by walking over to him and kissing him with all the tenderness I had in my heart. Breakfast be damned, I was going to show this man once again exactly how he made me feel—right there on the kitchen floor.

Although breakfast wasn't as good reheated, we managed to fuel ourselves and take a break from our obsessive lovemaking to get down to business. We still had some cleaning up to do before my sisters got home and I did want to go through more of Alessia's journal.

There wasn't much to tidy up in my room, aside from refolding a few clothes into the drawers and reorganizing my shoes and luggage in the closet. Doing a second check, I noted that nothing at all seemed to be missing or damaged—even my souvenirs were intact. Kieran volunteered to finish up downstairs in the setting area. He was still working on putting things back in place when I joined him.

"Anything missing from down here?"

"Not a thing, *a ghrá*. It's baffling. If they were looking for a person and got frustrated, they woulda just rummaged a few things on the way out the door. If they were lookin' to rob you, there's plenty worth taking to pawn for money. No, it was something specific on their mind, and I'm venturing he—or she—didn't find it."

Curious, indeed. But what Kieran said made sense. At least if he was right, that meant that we shouldn't be in any physical danger from the intruder. Looking around, it seemed like he had everything all back in place, until I saw the box of pictures I had brought down from the attic were overturned under the sofa. I took them out and started to assemble them back into the box, noticing a few were missing.

"Kieran look at this. Some of the photos we were looking at the other day aren't here anymore—like the one with Cian, Alessia and Lena. Do you think—"

Midsentence, he cut me off with a raise of his finger and rushed up the stairs to the attic. I followed him, understanding his hunch, already knowing what we would find. Sure enough, the tiny little loft was beyond trashed. Papers were everywhere, trinkets broken, boxes smashed. Someone was on a mission—a mission that involved a legacy I still didn't know anything about myself.

There was a hint of Irish temper boiling beneath his surface like a slow burning hotplate. He grabbed my arm forcefully and led me out of the attic and back down the stairs.

"Kieran, you're hurting me." He apologetically loosened his grip and moved his hand down to hold mine more gently, still moving rapidly to the setting area. He motioned for me to sit while he began pacing and mumbling a slew of what were probably Irish curses. He sounded a lot like Granny a few weeks ago.

"It's time, Megan. Call your sisters and have them come home. I'll get on Colleen and see when she can get here. There is a reason you are here and it's time she did the telling of it. I'm not liking this one bit. Not one bit, I tell you."

He walked towards the front door to have a word with the guard by the side garden and then called Colleen. Without alarming them, I convinced my sisters to come home early under the guise that Colleen was ready for us and after a long trip, didn't want to be up too late tonight.

Kieran came back in, still as wired as he was when he went out.

"I have some things I need to take care of right now, *a ghrá*. I need to check in on Mum, plus I need to have a little chat with the Commissioner to fill him in on what we learned. You're safe here with the guards. Colleen is on her way. I should be about two, three hours most. Did you get a hold of your sisters?"

"Yes, there is a ferry leaving in an hour that they can hop on. I told them Colleen was coming here earlier so they wouldn't be suspicious."

"Atta girl, good thinkin'. I hate leaving you like this, but I want to take care of business and return in time for the story. I don't mean to be intruding on your family business. But I can't protect you if I don't know all the facts."

"It's okay, I know. I want you there with me. My sisters will understand—they won't have a problem with it. You go ahead. I'll be just fine. I'll see you later." Moving a loose tendril of hair aside from his cheek, I leaned up to give him a kiss goodbye.

"I'll be back, Dream Rose," he said with a more relaxed tone, closing the door behind him.

I was grateful for the few hours to myself, truth be told. So much had happened over the last 48 hours—the last week—the last month! All my intentions to sift through my brain clutter had been tossed by the wayside in a tornado of unexpected events.

We learned about an unknown grandfather who abandoned our mother and grandmother. His dying wishes led us to Ireland and soon to Italy and Spain, on a wild goose chase for a few mysterious relics left to us in his will, and on a captivating mission to learn the legacies of our family's past. And now—with the break-in and missing photos—the stakes were seemingly higher than ever.

So much had been stirred up since coming here. The moment I stepped foot onto this sacred soil, I have felt both at home and lost. In the silence and peace, I have been challenged to find myself again and to finally heal the hurts of the past—to let go of the person I had let myself settle into.

Do I dare risk it all to write and travel and let those deepest dreams become a reality?

And then there is Kieran. Sweet, fierce, loving Kieran. I am carelessly getting swept up into this international intrigue that has to inevitably end, but I don't know if my heart can take the agony of letting him go. Oh dear God, am I falling in love with him?

How can that possibly be? I poke fun at those

incredulous dating shows that end in engagements after only a few months and shake my head at real-life proclaimed happily ever after stories. Yet here I was, knowing a man for a single week and considering the word "love" when I think of him.

It's absolutely ridiculous. I must be confusing lust with love. Idyllic romance with love. In my vulnerability and realization about Scotty, were my broken-down walls just grasping onto the first nice man who came my way?

How could I turn what is clearly a random holiday affair into something of substance? I barely know him. I just found out he likes his coffee black today, for goodness' sake. I only learned that he owned a pub last night and that he has a sensual singing voice this morning; one that he used to sing a song for me—a song that he wrote about me, no less.

Am I simply following his delusional lead? How could he possibly have the same deep feelings for me? Is he equally captivated only by the idea of being with some American girl on an enigmatic trip?

I knew I would drive myself crazy if I kept letting my mind ask all these questions. I don't think I am quite ready to confront this just yet. Yup, classic Meg avoidance. I decided to take out the journal again and distract myself with the love woes of an ancestor instead.

About an hour later, I heard the welcome sounds of my sisters bantering as they entered the house. *Hmm,* didn't they notice the armed guards outside? I took a quick peek to see Billy and Horace diligently hiding out of sight. I bet Kieran had something to do with that.

Happy to be surrounded by their familiar faces, I ran to the front door to greet them with big hugs.

"Hey! How was your trip? I want to hear all about it!"

Tropical storm Marissa was eager to spill the details. Leaving her luggage right near the door, she plopped down on the couch in excitement. Mia resigned to do the same but was more cautious about it.

Uh oh, her CSI antennas were up—damn it.

I put on my best game face, bringing in tea and some of the fruit salad I had made from this morning as I listened to Marissa gush about their Clare Island experience.

"It was fantastic! Oh, I wish you would have been there with us! We stayed right within the lighthouse in this adorable little room with a view overlooking the sea. It was so tranquil, unlike anywhere I've ever been! Everyone dined together like a big family each night. The service made us feel like royalty. And then we went to the yoga center and got all zen.

"Oh, we split up for some alone time too, so I went on one of those bike hikes while Mia traveled down to the town's shops and then I think spent most of her day in the lighthouse's library, right? It was great to get away. I feel rejuvenated," she ended with a big sigh to indicate she was done and ready to come up for air.

"That does sound amazing and relaxing." I looked over at Mia, who was growing more anxious and uncomfortable by the minute. "What's wrong, Mia? Didn't you enjoy yourself?"

"Oh, I did. Very much. It's not that."

"Then what is it?"

"You tell me," she said accusingly.

Nervous, I shifted in my seat and took a sip of tea. *Shit, I knew it.*

"What do you mean?"

"Come on, Meg. I'm not stupid. You call us to cut our trip short with some story about Colleen needing to meet us earlier—she's a pocketful of energy, late owl type, so what's the big rush all of a sudden? Plus, you've been jumpy since the minute we walked through the door.

"You think I don't notice the officers standing in the back of the garden? Give me a little credit. Wife of a cop, remember?"

"Can't get anything past you."

"No, you can't. Now tell us—what the hell has been going on around here?"

"Okay," I took a deep breath, not knowing exactly where to start. I led them through the first day when I decided to go up to the attic and found the box of photos and diary. I filled them in on what I learned about our ancestors so far. I left out the part about Kieran joining me for now—I'd get to that later.

Then they sat wide-eyed and worried as I recounted how I felt like I was being followed when I went to the market and then after taking a walk to the creek, how I found the house in shambles.

"Wow, who would do such a thing?" asked Marissa incredibly.

"Well, Kieran and I seem to think that it could be related to our family inheritance, since a few pictures were the only thing they took."

"Wait—how does Kieran fit into all this?" Mia caught on quick.

"Well, that's the other thing," I relented, ready to spill the beans. "We've gotten closer."

"How close?" They asked almost in accord, like a staggered echo.

I started my next round of storytelling, hardly able to contain the pure bliss of finding my own pot of gold. Knowing they'd somehow get it out of me anyway, I told them everything their hungry little ears wanted to hear about our delicious entanglement.

"I'm so happy for you—and relieved he was here to help!" said Mia, with Marissa concurring.

"Me too. I honestly don't know what I would have done without him here. He's the one who set up the guards, helped me translate some of this journal and is now working on who knows what to keep us safe.

"If it is okay with you," I began nervously, "he'd like to come back and hear what Colleen has to say to see if it helps him figure out some pieces to the puzzle. I know this is a private family matter, but he's all wrapped up in this now. But only if you are on board with it."

"Of course," obliged Mia. "I like the fact that someone local is here to look out for us, especially when we have no idea who or what we are up against."

"Yeah, sure," said Marissa quietly, but I could tell there was a hesitation in her voice. I dismissed it, knowing her well enough to recognize that the little hint of jealously over my special overseas adventure played a part in it. I knew she was genuinely happy for me, but she would be happier if she had her own love affair going on at the same time. Weird—because I thought she did.

"Thank you. He should be back in another hour, about the time I expect Colleen to arrive. I'd like to read a little more in this journal first. Do you want to join me?"

"Actually, I'm feeling unsettled from hearing all this and need some time to think. You know how I get—I'd really like to go lose myself in the kitchen and make us all a wonderful dinner before we talk. We do have some food in there, right?" I laughed at Mia as I nodded my head in consent.

"How about you, Marissa?"

"Same with me. I think I'd like to take a walk."

"I don't think that is a good idea with everything going on. We should stay together where the guards are until we know we are safe."

Reluctantly, she agreed. "Fine. I'll just go out and walk around the backyard for a bit—in the guard's view," she added.

"Hey," I called to her, as she turned around in obvious frustration. "I love you, Mar."

She smiled meekly, but it was at least a smile. "I love you too, big sis."

12

The air was filled with the scents of Mia's Guinness beef stew and soda bread. I could hear my stomach rumbling before it unceremoniously turned to flutters when Kieran walked in.

"It smells grand in here!" he exclaimed with hungry enthusiasm as he made his way towards me, then hesitated.

"It's fine. They know."

Relieved, he pulled me in for an affectionate kiss hello. Time did him some good—he was back to his agreeable self again. He greeted both my sisters and then Colleen, who arrived only a few minutes earlier. She was busy in the kitchen helping Mia set up as she rambled on about her latest crisis, glad to have an ear in my sympathetic sister.

"What have you been up to?" I asked him.

"I promised Mum to help her run a few errands. She's getting on in the years and though she can't be kept from her kitchen, she's having a hard time with the keeping of the house and whatnot. Her friend Gerty popped over for a visit, so she scooted me out—but not before she yanked some info out of me about where I'd been," he grinned. "She hopes to be meeting you before you leave."

"That would be nice. I'd love to." Meet his mother? The panic moved through me like the oxygen masks had unexpectedly popped down in a turbulent airplane. Not sure which life-risking situation I'd rather be in right now. This was moving way too fast, like my brakes were tampered with and I couldn't stop the speeding car.

"Dinner's ready!" came the call from the kitchen to break my panic attack.

She had outdone herself again, I thought, taking a bite into a tender morsel of beef. Dinner was full of frivolous conversation, sharing our tourist tales, learning even more places that we "must see" according to Colleen and hearing all about the pub locals from Kieran.

But underneath it all was the underlying tension of what the evening was really all about. When dinner was done, it was Colleen who was the first to break the silence.

"Shall we retreat to the setting area? Kieran, be a good lad and get the fire goin', would ya?"

Sat and settled, not even a creak from the old house dared to break the hush that fell over us as we anxiously awaited what our cousin had to reveal.

"Now mind you, I'm only allowed to be tellin' you about the ring legacy. Still don't understand the way of all the tellin', though," she muttered to the side.

"Anyways, the story of the O'Sullivans dates way back, quite a few generations where they be of royal blood livin' just outside the Pale. That'd be Dublin," she advised.

"Now over many a donkey's years, wars and whatnot pushed our ancestors to settle across the way in County Cork. Though they were no longer in line for the crown, they were still mighty noble with all their riches, they were. Many lived on in peace and prosperity for a good yard of time as such.

"Back in those days, there was no mixin' of the blood, as they would call it. That would have been a holy show for sure! Had to be pure Irish through and through, they did. That is, until your great-great-great grandparent's generation.

"Banan O'Sullivan was the babe of seven children and hardly an heir, but still all posh enough, as it were. One day, his da—that would be James O'Sullivan—met a Spanish nobleman, Eduardo Rubio, whose family had just fallen from grace, thanks to his dosser of a father. That eejit cost the Rubios their honorable status. Didn't have the full shilling, if you know what I mean," she hinted as she circled her fingers around her head in a "cuckoo bird" motion.

She then paused to reprimand herself for not sticking properly to her intended narrative. "Of course, the story of the Rubios has to be the tellin' of *someone else* when you get to Barcelona. All these rules with the tellin'. Egads."

"It's fine," I said as I placed my hand on her arm and smiled. "I love the way you are telling your chosen story. Please continue."

With a grand grin, she resumed her tale to tell.

"An arrangement was made for Rubio's youngwan, Elena, to marry our Banan so that she would be well taken care of and not livin' in bits. Being that Banan was the youngest of seven, who he was hitched to made no matter to his da. Jammy for Rubio, indeed, the lucky bastard.

"It was reckoned a fierce match, though the two forced lovebirds were not so tickled to lob the gob and join in marriage. Elena had to give up all she had known in Spain to move here, she did.

"They were both given a savage fortune for the deal, though. Since staying with his four older brothers on the O'Sullivan family land would be biscuits to a bear, they decided to move away and settle in County Mayo—

landing right here in this very gaff.

"It was a purely rural area back then, but Banan—that cute hoor—had the means to build their home upon this land, along with several other homes and businesses. It's how the chancer made his own fortune, don'tcha know. Of course, those properties have since been sold off to pay for various debts of certain gammy heirs, mind you," she lamented.

Hmm—so I wasn't far off about this town being built like a Monopoly board, with our multi-great grandfather being Uncle Moneybags. Interesting.

"After a while of the marriage, Banan and Elena formed a proper kinship and were rather taken with each other. It is said they were a lovely couple; kind and generous to all. They got on brilliantly—had a grand life, ya know. Well, she bore him two lads: Banan Junior and Cian.

"I'm goin' to just call him Junior so there's no making a haymes of the two Banans," she pointed out, as we nodded in appreciation for the clarity.

"When Junior was born, Banan the elder presented Elena with his mum's treasured ring, which he himself had received in secret upon her death. The story goes that Agatha O'Sullivan had a mighty big soft spot for her wee little one, and so he became the chosen one to inherit the sacred family jewel.

"One of them original Claddagh rings from the 1700's—a one-of-a-kind, never-made-again type. The *Legacy of Love Claddagh*, it be called. Here," she said, handing me an old, tattered picture she took out from her purse.

"It's striking," was all I could muster to describe what I saw. It was a gold Claddagh-style ring with a Celtic knot braid around the band and a solitary emerald sitting upon its center in the shape of a heart, a border of tiny white diamonds caressing its delicate outline.

Not particularly a jewelry person by nature, I fell in love with the exquisitely designed sphere. It called to me just like everything else in this country. Passing the photo around the room, my sisters were equally impressed.

"It was said to be branded in the name of love, it was. But more on that later. Let's not stall the ball," she gestured hastily, eager to carry on.

"So, Banan Junior got the ring from his mother, Agatha?" Marissa asked, perplexed by the complicated history.

"No, no, that wasn't the way of it. Let me back it up. Now, follow along.

"Agatha got the ring when she married James O'Sullivan, who inherited it from his mum and so on. And since Agatha's babe, Banan *the First*, proved to be a dear fella to his foreign betrothed, Elena Rubio, she felt it right to pass it on to him above the others. When Banan *the First* realized his love for Elena and their newborn son *Junior*, he was buzzin' to make it hers. It was then Elena's jewel for keeps."

Colleen courteously paused for Marissa's light bulb of acknowledgment to go off. "Got it."

"Now, as I said, there be two boys from them. Junior and Cian. Well, Junior was a bit of a spoiled scallywag, if you ask me. Entitled little twit, I heard. And I could believe it, because he be my own grandfather—and not the warm type neither.

"He married into another rich family, takin' Kira Callaghan as his wife. Another prize if you ask me. Snooty grandma. I hated when my da made us pay a visit. Sorry,

I'll carry on. They had Banan III—me da—and Teagan O'Sullivan, me auntie. All these Banans—I'll just call me da 'Three.'

"Are you keepin' up with me, lasses?"

"Actually, I think so." She grinned when she saw me writing away in my own journal like a *New York Times* reporter covering a big scoop.

"Ah, now that's smarts. Well done, cuz. You found yourself a good match, Kieran, if you don't mind my saying."

He beamed warmly as he pressed his lips into the top of my head. "I did indeed."

Colleen continued with her elongated diatribe about how Junior was a "wile slabber," causing trouble wherever he went. As the rumor goes, he was envious of his younger brother, Cian, whose somewhat better looks and even better disposition earned him a lot of respect in the community—until his dalliance with Italian-born Alessia Bianchi.

Junior tried to use the scandal to his advantage to nudge his baby brother completely out of the way, but his parents would have none of it. Colleen apologized for getting ahead of herself again, cursing that she had to stop the story there because she'd never get to the "real of it" if she kept going off on her tangents.

She resumed the family tree lineup: "Three," her da, married a lovely woman named Mary Collins and had Colleen and her brother Shane. The Collins were with whom she lived with now, as they were the only family she had left after her brother's passing.

Her auntie Teagan also went on to marry well—to a man named Harry Walsh. Tragically, she could not have children. So Colleen, who had never been married or had children herself, is now the last in that line of O'Sullivans, she explained.

On the other O'Sullivan line, Cian and Alessia, despite all the protest and shame they faced, married and had Lena, who then married the wealthy and ambitious Antonio Marino for money.

"Poor lass," Colleen bemoaned. "Her heart was broke to the bone by Ian McDonough, her true love, when he honored his da's wish for an arranged marriage to another mot."

Colleen then revealed how Lena was so crushed and devoid of faith that she ultimately gave up on love and chose to marry for money instead—despite Alessia's attempts to steer her daughter back towards her heart.

But Antonio was madly in love with Lena, and perhaps his inability to take no for an answer wore her already weakened heart down to submission. She subsequently bore two sons, Leigh and firstborn Antonio Jr., who sadly died at the tender age of seven from smallpox.

From there, Leigh married Lillith, and supposedly had no children before divorcing her and marrying his original betrothed, Julia, and adopting her son as his own.

"I always thought I was the end of the O'Sullivan line—aside from Leigh, of course. I thought my cousin was slaggin' me when he called me about the ring and confessed about his Alissa. Scarlet I was after giving him some lashin' for lyin' and then it bein' the bang on truth after all.

"But there you have the whole of it."

Feeling satisfied that we were all caught up on the family tree, Colleen then shifted back to the history of the ring, saying that because of Junior's poor behavior and the difficulty the scandal brought upon the star-crossed lovers, Elena bequeathed the *Legacy of Love Claddagh* ring to Cian and Alessia instead. She supported their love and their fight to be together and believed the ring represented everything their marriage stood for.

Apparently, that didn't sit well with Junior, who protested but lost the fight in the end. He instead was satisfied with many other riches that weren't as sentimental in value, despite his wife Kira's continued objections.

"I remember Grandmum Kira eating the head off Granda one day, saying he was a right moran for not nabbing some ring out of Great Auntie Alessia's bag. I happened to be earwiging under the kitchen table, and they didn't even know it. I did that a lot," she chuckled mischievously.

But the ring remained in Cian and Alessia's possession, Colleen attested, until it was ready to be passed down to Lena as their love child. Even though Lena did not live with love for her husband, the purity of her love for her children and her loyalty to her family made her worthy enough in Alessia's eyes to inherit it—with the promise to keep it secretly away from Antonio and the Marino family. She had faith in her daughter's heart, and that was enough.

Lena held onto the sacred band, hoping that her son would be the one to once again honor its true symbolism, given its rich history and meaning. By then, she had regretted her own life choices and vowed to restore the deep meaning of love back into this legacy.

She secretly cheered with pride as her son, Leigh, ran away to marry his true love Lillith, even against the family's wishes. However, she was not convinced of his strength to keep his promise to stay away from the family, and so kept the ring a secret.

Lena originally intended to bequeath it to Colleen as a true O'Sullivan, but with no family to pass it onto herself, Colleen had no objection to it all working out this way.

"Fair play, it is. All is as it should be," Colleen declared before she explained how it all went down.

When Lena was dying, as Leigh told Colleen, he had confessed everything to his mother about his love for Lillith and the secret daughter they shared. It was then that Lena revealed the existence of the ring, and an accompanying letter that tells of its origins.

She finally believed he was ready to receive his rightful treasures and keep them safe—all of them.

She urged him to continue to keep the ring silent from the Marinos—made him take an oath to pass it along to his true family when the time came. That was one vow he did not break.

He never told the Marinos of this ring, of its meaning or of its value. Designed for royalty, today it was worth hundreds of thousands of dollars.

"How can that be?" Marissa interrupted. "I didn't realize that emeralds could be worth so much."

"Oh, that ain't no emerald, lass. That be a rare green diamond."

The room became more silent than a Charlie Chaplin movie. A few minutes passed before I spoke.

"Where is the ring now and why would our grandfather pass it down to me and not to Mia, if it's a ring that represents love? She's the married one of the family. Or better yet—why not to our mother?"

"Ay lass, I wondered that myself. When Leigh and I spoke, he was acting the maggot, saying that he had other plans for his Alissa. He crafted quite the deadly strategy for this legacy after studying you all since you were wee babes. It wasn't haphazard, I can tell you that. Blows my mind to think of all the planning involved. Fine thing, he was."

Her voice was filled with genuine awe.

"Anyway, he knew that you had the romantic spirit of his grandmum. You were undoubtedly, to him, the rightful Celtic *dúchas* and being such, he knew it would be meant for you."

Looking from me to Kieran, she commented, "By the looks of it, sure seems he placed it in the right hands."

I blushed and could feel Kieran heat up a bit as well. Were we really that transparent? It was just an affair, for goodness' sake. Not something worth earning an extravagantly expensive ring for. Holy crap—hundreds of thousands of dollars.

"It be held in a lockbox down in Dublin. You'll be needing to take your next trip there to see Quinn Clark, who will be doing all kinds of verification stuff before sending you to the bank for the lockbox."

"Colleen, may I ask why there is all this mystery surrounding the ring? I mean, why keep it a secret and have us go through such lengths to pass it down through the generations?" asked Mia.

"It be richer than millions, lass—in legend more so than even money. It carries with it a blessing of love and there ain't nothing richer than that in this world. In the wrong hands, it could be melted down to nothing and sold. In the right hands, it will live on, as will its legacy."

"I promise to treasure it always. I will protect it and pass it along to the right person when my time comes," I said, choking up. "I am so honored to be chosen for this."

Marissa interrupted the moment to remind us of

something important: did this ring have something to do with someone breaking into the house and stealing the photos?

"That be a mystery to me, for sure. As Leigh told it, I was the only one he was tellin' the truth to about the ring—not even his family or his lawyer. It was just a trinket to them, he supposed, so best be leavin' it that way so you'd get no push back.

"I didn't know anything about it a'tall until Lena reached out, except like I said, I did sometimes hear Grandmum Kira rumble about a ring that was rightfully hers not bein' hers, but that didn't last too long. Lots of baubles later and I'm sure she got over it. And I'm the only one left on this side for the O'Sullivans, so there be no put off ancestors over here."

"Do you think there could be any unknown heirs in your line who might know about this legacy? Or maybe even—who was the first lady again? Oh, Agatha. Perhaps there is someone interested from her side of the family; the one before she married into the O'Sullivan's."

"I suppose there could be," she considered thoughtfully. "I suppose we could even join in Grandmum Kira's line if we wanted to, if she kept rattlin' on about it. But remember, this ring has been a secret in our family for generations and as I heard it, swearings of secrecy accompanied the tellin' of it. Though not sure how much coulda been leaked from me grumpy old grandies, so anything is possible, I'd wager. I can write up my own extended family tree if it helps."

"It would. Thank you," I replied.

"Do you remember when Mr. Perkins told us that one of the family members—oh what's her name?—was curious about protesting this?" Marissa recalled. "What if she is behind it?"

"Peggy Marino? Patrick's wife? I guess we shouldn't rule out anyone at this point. We can have Kevin check in with the authorities at home," I said. "It seems like the more people who are exposed to this legacy, the more suspects to consider."

"Which reminds me," interjected Colleen. "All of you in this room, including you, Mr. MacGovern, breaking the rules as an outsider—you must vow that you will not speak of this to anyone beyond these here walls. The next person to hear this story, Megan, should be the heir of it."

"I understand. But what about my mother and grandmother? They are part of this heritage. May I share this additional information with them?" I thought it would only be fair, since it should have been in their possession all along.

"Ay of course, but just be careful in the tellin' that it ends there. Never know who be earwiging out there, lookin' to start trouble."

"I promise, I will be very careful. Only my mother and grandmother. No one else."

"Right then. I'm a bit flogged. Would ye be mindin' if I stayed over the night?"

"Not at all. You are welcome to stay as long as you'd like," said Mia. "And please do not fight me on this—I insist you take my room tonight. I can stay in with Megan."

"I won't be fightin' you tonight, lass. Thank you."

"In fact," I announced, "I think we should all be turning in. We learned a lot tonight and we should just sleep on it. We can figure it all out in the morning—including our trip to Dublin."

Nodding in agreement, we pitched in to tidy up the kitchen before retiring. I hated seeing Kieran leave after knowing what it was like to wake up in his arms, but I knew this would be for the best. Besides, I thought as I kissed him goodbye, we could both use a night of *actual* sleep.

Early in the morning, the preparations for Dublin began. We each took our parts—Mia on transportation and hotel duty and Marissa on touristy must-sees. I called to make arrangements to meet with Quinn Clark later in the afternoon.

This whole trip was turning out to be one big tumultuous journey. Part of me was looking forward to going back home to normalcy. Thank goodness we already planned to wait two months before taking our next trip to Italy. I was exhausted just thinking about it.

With not much time to spare, we boarded the train to Dublin after bidding Colleen a sad goodbye. I had to settle for a "see you in a few days" call with Kieran, sullenly realizing that I only had four more days before I left him for good.

Oh, how my heart and body ached for him like the desert for water. I wish he had been able to join us, but I knew this was a sister trip and I needed to honor that. These were going to be the longest two days of my life until I saw him again.

But maybe that was a good thing—maybe I should cut the ties now since I was leaving soon anyway. Go cold turkey. Just let that one amazing night be the best memory of my life and not complicate it any further. It would be better that way, I decided. It had to be that way, for both of our own good.

The train ride was humdrum, with my sisters and I

remaining relatively quiet except for a few whispered exchanges of insight into what we had learned about the ring and our family history. I was more anxious than anyone to find out what kind of verification Quinn Clark needed and what awaited us in Dublin.

Kieran made his objection to the trip without him or police protection known, but we assured him that we were three strong women who would be fine. We let him arrange for a guard to take us to the train depot and then had one awaiting us at Dublin to escort us to our hotel. I was starting to get annoyed with the whole macho overprotective thing.

How did I ever survive life without it? I sarcastically questioned.

Dublin was a bustling city—the complete opposite of that old-world little town in County Mayo. After we checked into our hotel rooms, we realized we had a few hours before my meeting with Mr. Clark, so we decided to lighten things up with some sightseeing.

We stopped in the National Gallery of Ireland for Marissa, who was particularly enamored with the Monet and Italian painters exhibits. Of course, in the gift shop, she found several books on Goya she just *had* to have.

After exiting the museum, we strolled through the city's famous Merrion Square. I grinned broadly when I saw the dedicated Oscar Wilde statue in one of the park's corners and nodded in credit to the powers that be for sending me their not-so-subtle sign in the form of the very quote Kieran first seduced me with.

I took a picture of it and sent it off to him to let him know I was thinking of him.

Quinn Clark's office was tiny but meticulously kept, a single suite on the third floor of a large Dublin office building not far off from the Square. He was a short, stout man, balding with a thick mustache and ruby red cheeks. A genial character, he greeted us warmly, exclaiming how he was awaiting our arrival.

"May I offer you some tea?" asked the young, red-haired beauty with emerald eyes and perfectly manicured hands. I assumed it was his assistant.

"That would be lovely, thank you," remembering that here, it is more polite to accept than decline.

"Please come sit down," offered Mr. Clark. "It's a pleasure to meet you all. Now which of you be Megan Rossi?"

"That would be me," I said, extending out my hand in welcome before sitting down. The visit was rather routine; he simply needed to check my passport to confirm I was the correct sister, take a sample of my DNA with a swab of the inside of my cheek and have me sign some papers releasing the lockbox to me.

He told me that he should have the approval by morning and would then provide me with the bank's address after exchanging the proper clearances.

"That went better than I anticipated," confessed Marissa. "I half expected another riddle to be solved before getting to the damn bank."

"We haven't gotten there yet, so don't jinx us," I kidded. "Well, we have plenty of time to kill this evening and probably in the morning before we hear back. What's your fancy?"

They looked at each other with a signal of agreement. "The Guinness Storehouse!"

We made it into the Storehouse right before closing, as luck would have it. We had just enough time to go on a self-guided tour, learning how to pour a perfect pint before enjoying one on the house. The free sample took us way up to the seventh floor to the Gravity Bar, a circular room with wide-open glass windows revealing a 360-degree panoramic view of the city.

We were so engrossed in the moment that we failed to notice a man hidden among the crowded lounge area watching us carefully.

"Ladies, I don't know about you, but this has been the experience of a lifetime. I'm so glad to be sharing it with you both," said Mia as she raised her glass in a toast.

"Oh, it's been a dream come true. All this art and history—it makes me sad to see it come to an end soon," shared Marissa.

"Me too," said a familiar voice. I turned around to find Kieran standing right behind me with his own pint and that sexy smirk.

"Kieran! What—what are you doing here?"

"That was all me," said Mia with pride. "I asked him to come here to be with you. It didn't seem right for you to be apart with so few days left here."

"Not that I am not thrilled to see you," I said, then turning to my sisters, "but this is our family adventure. It's supposed to be about us."

"It *is* about us. But it is also about *you*," Mia pointed out. "This is your particular journey, in Ireland, with this ring. Every experience you have here is a part of the big picture. That includes Kieran."

"Excuse us a moment?" I pulled Mia to the side, leaving behind a confused Kieran and a perturbed Marissa.

Whispering, I began to scold her. "What are you doing? You have no right to meddle in my business like this. It's unfair to Kieran. It has to stop."

"Why, Megan? Why does this have to stop? It doesn't

take a genius to see that he is genuinely crazy about you—and you about him. I have not seen you glow like this, like ever—not even with Scotty. Are you telling me that you are okay with just walking away from this—from something you may never find again for the rest of your life?"

"Yes. No. I mean, I don't know. I'm so confused, Mia."

"I know, I get it. I didn't mean to push. But don't you owe it to yourself and to that man over there to honestly see what this is?"

I tossed her a slight head bob as a gesture she could be right.

"There's a reason I booked separate rooms for us all tonight. I suggest you take advantage of it," she advised in that maternal, no-nonsense tone of hers, walking away back towards the rest of our group.

"All settled," Mia announced in cocky triumph.

13

It took less than a minute after closing the hotel door behind us before Kieran began ravishing me. Clothes fell to the floor in rushed desire—the kisses were hard and zealous instead of the gentle, loving ones leading the way on our first night together.

"Not being with you last night drove me crazy."

"Tell me about it," he whispered hoarsely. "I must have taken a dozen cold showers."

He continued to kiss me hard, deeply, as he grabbed my breasts and began toying with my nipples to stir me up. I curved under his touch, bringing his body closer to mine. His hand moved rapidly down my side and into me, satisfied to find me moist and ready for him. He slipped inside so naturally, his thrusts hurried with mutual longing.

"Not so fast," I smiled naughtily, turning him over so that I could take control. I wanted to know what it felt like to ride him like a Harley Davidson, to feel that rush of adrenaline against my open road. I decided to start out slowly, moving ever so seductively and building up the intensity between us.

I ignored his pleas of wanting more, yearning to go faster, but that made it all the more exciting for me to take my time. When I knew neither of us couldn't resist any longer, I moved more forcefully, skillfully rocking with increasing speed. With each passionate lunge, I could feel both of us rising to the heights of ecstasy until we simultaneously exploded into an orgasmic wonderland of love and lust.

I held onto the electric shivers that coursed through my entire body, pausing to let the release flow through me completely into an uncontrollable shudder before curling up in his sweaty, loving arms. I knew then it would be another delightfully sleepless night.

Morning came too soon, and the hint of sunlight from the window reminded me that this couldn't be some lazy day in bed—there was a lot to be done. Looking over at my beautiful man lying there asleep, I soundlessly left the bed so I could get into the shower. Not long after, Kieran had awoken and snuck in to join me, distracting me once again from my mission in the most pleasing of ways.

We finally were able to pull ourselves apart and get dressed. He ordered up some breakfast, which I had forgotten about, while I checked my phone to see if there were any messages from Mr. Clark. I was hoping the results would have been in by this point. Not realizing that I was being watched, I looked up to find Kieran staring at me with an amused smile.

"What?"

"Do you know how incredibly adorable you are when you pout in frustration?"

I could only shake my head at him, moving over to the bed to sit on his lap for a full body embrace and kiss. Although I was laughing, I noticed he became a bit more thoughtful and the air in the room shifted from playful to serious.

"I could hold you like this for the rest of my life, *mo shíorghrá.*"

My body immobilized in place. Freezing superseded

fright or flight, leaving my instincts clouded as to what to say or do next.

"What did you just call me?"

"*Mo shíorghrá*. It means—"

"I know exactly what it means," I interrupted crossly as I leapt off his lap and walked over to the other side of the room to let my brain take over for my foolish heart.

'My Eternal Love.' What Leigh called Granny. His broken promises, her crushed heart and the end of a true love all came rushing back to me. Just like Scotty and his own empty words. Another sworn road that led to nowhere.

It was the wakeup call I needed that this had gotten too serious, too fast, and that it needed to end now before it went any further. I should have fought harder against Mia's suggestion to live in the moment and insisted that Kieran return home. Look where it's gotten me now.

I've been lovestruck stupid. *This* is exactly why I tried my damnedest for years to rid myself of my own quixotic nature. It's a drug that pulls me in and makes me hopelessly delusional.

I am only here for two weeks; it's not real. This is not some simulated sentimental movie I'm starring in. It's just some overseas flirtation. *Jesus, Megan. Are you that daft?*

I know better than this. My vow be damned—I was in over my head with this butterfly transformation of soul nakedness. This is not what I committed myself to on those cliffs. His seemingly harmless sweet talk reminded me that I was only conning myself that we could play the role of everlasting lovers.

"Whoa, Megan—why are you so angry?" He looked truly bewildered.

"I'm not angry—I'm just—I'm just frustrated. Mostly with myself. Kieran, we've known each other, what, a week? And you are dropping endearments of eternal love? Come on, Gov."

"It's how I feel, Meg. What's gotten into you?" I saw the look of pain in his eyes and had to turn away.

"It's just—" I paused for a moment, not knowing what to say. Usually so composed, I couldn't find the right words. "This is not a fairy tale, Kieran. Flowery language may have gotten me into bed, but it's not going to keep this, whatever this is, going. It's so—trite sounding," I blurted.

Looking utterly baffled, I could see a bit of temper flaring beneath his volcanic surface. "Sorry, I don't just drop meaningless flatteries to get a woman into bed. That's not who I am, and you should at least know that by now. I meant every word I've ever said to you."

"Yeah well, that's what Granny thought too before my grandfather up and abandoned her. I won't be another victim of Irish blarney."

"Ah, so that's the story, is it? It's about your granda? You gotta be kidding me."

"No, I'm serious. Who's to say that you wouldn't do the same thing to me the second I board the plane?" As soon as the sassy words came out, I knew I hit a nerve, but held firm to my defiance. I had to cement my mindset.

You are in a meeting with Jones and he is trying to usurp you, I told myself, recreating an old work adversary scenario. *Gain your emotional balance and rise above his persuasion. You are the influencer. You call the shots.*

Full on angry now, Kieran marched over to where I was, grabbed me by the arms and looked straight into my eyes with fury as he spat, "I am not your grandfather.

Don't ever compare me to another man like that."

He stood strong, holding on, as we matched fire with fire. Finally, he released his grasp when I let a wince sneak out, but he didn't budge from his place right up against my face.

"Fine, then let's just talk about you—this," I gestured, pushing him back to give myself space. I couldn't look at him any longer. My resolve was diminishing quickly, and I knew I had to be strong for my own self-preservation. One of us had to be logical about all this. Guess that would have to be me.

What good would this relationship do when I returned to New York? That was the fundamental question that had to be addressed. That's what this ultimately comes down to. Time to face what we were both in denial about.

"This has all been wonderful, but I think this has gone far enough," I finally said matter-of-factly. "I'm leaving in two days, so there is no point in dragging this out, Kieran. It's time to end this little love game, don't you think?"

Stunned at the change in personality, he mumbled something inaudible before addressing me.

"What game? Who's playing a game? Have you lost your mind? Who *are* you?" he asked as he exasperatingly ran his fingers through his hair in disbelief. He legitimately looked taken aback. "I'm not playing any games here, Megan. If anyone be playing at something, it's you, out of nowhere. I don't even know this woman standing here in front of me."

"Well, it's time you met the *true* Meg, then. The smart and sensible one. Not the scared, helpless, silly girl you seem to fancy."

"Believe it or not, I fancy *all* of you," he barely managed through gritted teeth.

"No, what you love is the drama of it all. Since the day we met, it's been non-stop romantic gestures and surprises and all kinds of courting. For what? We shouldn't be talking and acting like it's love when we just met because truthfully, it's not going anywhere.

"Can't we just call it what it is, some really great sex, and move on?" I felt the scorpion sting go right through his heart, instantly regretting the words.

"Feck, woman, really great sex? Is that what *you* think this was?"

I might have gone a bit too far. I couldn't backtrack now, though. What's done is done. I had to be the director and call end scene. Now or never—before my nerves of steel dwindled.

Still, it killed me inside to see him hurting like this; to know I was the one hurting him. I'd be lying to myself if I said this felt right. It didn't. But ending this now was the only thing that made sense in the big picture. Clearly, he wasn't on the same page.

"I didn't ask to meet you. I didn't ask to fall in love with you. I didn't ask for any of this, Meg. But here it is, clear as day and I can't stop or control what I feel."

"You just met me. It's not real. It's just—lust," I barely managed, still trying to convince myself more than him.

I started to weaken. I was fighting so hard against the feelings, against my own growing love for him, but it just can't be. We're from two different worlds, literally. I live in another country, for goodness' sake.

"Don't you dare tell me what I mean and what I don't mean, lass."

He grabbed me and kissed me more vehemently than he ever did before. My body couldn't help but override my mind and respond, feeling the heat that was so natural between us, mixed with the sweetness of two souls that were connected by more than just kisses.

"Does that feel like just lust?" he pleaded in a raspy, broken voice.

As I stood there fighting against the tears, speechless without a sharp comeback, his temper took a backseat. He gently lifted my chin up for our eyes to meet, with sincere concern and even the threat of his own tears lining his eyes.

"Do you mind telling me what this is really all about, lass?"

I took a moment to gather my scrambled thoughts.

"I feel like I am all caught up in some girlish love fantasy and I don't need this complication in my life right now." Perhaps straight up honesty might be the ticket to get me off this merry-go-round.

We sat in silence for a moment until I felt stronger to resume. He was giving me the chance to explain myself, which made him all the more difficult to resist. Ugh. How am I going to get through this sensibly with those eyes on me?

Be resilient, Meg. You can do this.

"I have worked my ass off to get where I am in life. I have fought against a corporate America where men are more respected, and I have had to claw my way with as much dignity as I could to earn half the respect. I am independent and can take care of myself, Kieran. What we have enjoyed has been truly fantastic, but it's not this Disney-esque love affair that needs to extend beyond this trip.

"Although I appreciate your concern, I also don't need some man protecting me as if I can't handle myself. I hate who I have been, feeling like this feeble female needing some knight on a white horse. I'm a strong woman, damn it, not a victim. And I certainly don't need to fall into the arms of a man and forget who I am. I won't lose myself ever again—not for anyone."

He paused for a while, taking in everything I said before he got up. His back stiffened, standing away from me, inhaling deeply. He sensed I was not going to budge. He then turned around and spoke sharply.

"I love you for exactly the woman you are, Megan Rossi. I love that you're independent and can take care of yourself. I love that we can match wits. I love your fire and everything that makes you, you. The bad-ass executive and the whimsical writer.

"I love *all* of it. So much so that I wanted to keep you safe. Not to be sexist and diminish your strength, but to preserve it. I love you, against my own wishes, feck it, but I do. It was truly instant for me. Why can't you accept that?"

"Because it can't be," I concluded in a defeated whisper. "We got swept up in the moment. It's time for us to just let it go before either of us gets hurt."

"Too late. Forgive me for misreading your signs that you felt as strongly for me as I felt for you. But if a fling is all you wanted, you got it. Thanks for the great sex," he hissed back bitterly, as he walked out the door and slammed it.

All I could do was just sink down into the corner on the floor, dumbfounded.

What have I done? What the fuck is wrong with you, Megan?

I then let the sobs fall out until I was a completely crumpled ragdoll of a mess.

Gratefully, my pity party didn't last too long. Mr. Clark called soon after with the news that I was cleared to pick up the ring from the bank. I took a few minutes to pull myself together, covering up the evidence that I had a long morning of crying before seeing my sisters.

I also had to come up with a good cover story about why Kieran was no longer there—I just didn't have it in me to listen to them rattle on about their own fantasies about us. I'm not sure if they bought the story that he had to go back to his mum to help her out, but it was enough to keep the questions at a minimum—at least for now.

The trip to the bank was surprisingly just as smooth as our meeting with Mr. Clark. With some simple identification, I was handed the keys to the safe deposit box and led to a private room for us to view its contents. Inside was a small metal fireproof box that had certainly seen some wear and tear over its many years.

Opening it up, we were collectively stunned at the pure exquisiteness of the ring I held in my hand. The picture had not done it justice. Although it could use a bit of a cleaning, you could tell it was well preserved over the many generations.

"The *Legacy of Love Claddagh* ring. Wow. It's absolutely stunning," I whispered in awe.

"I'll say. Try it on—does it fit?" Marissa asked.

"It's a little loose. I guess I'll need to get it fitted, though I'm not sure I'm really worthy of wearing it, despite our grandfather's faith in me."

"Why would you say that?" Mia asked.

"Kieran didn't really go home to check on his mum."

"We already suspected that," confessed Marissa. "Are you ready to tell us why he did leave?"

"We got into a fight. He called me *mo shíorghrá* like Leigh called Granny and I don't know—it just triggered me. All the pain came rushing back from Scotty falsely promising to love me forever and seeing Granny's broken heart and thinking about the impossibility of living in two different countries—I just—I couldn't let all this nonsense go on. So, I put an end to it. It didn't end very well."

"Oh Meg, I'm so sorry." Mia gave me a big hug. Marissa, on the other hand, was just staring at me incredulously.

"So you mean to tell me, that after all this time, you find someone you could actually love, who loves you like crazy back, and your response is to run away?"

"Marissa!" scolded Mia.

"No. Don't chide me like I'm the one in the wrong here. Meg, we have watched you struggle for years to get over Scotty. And then we saw you have this wonderful epiphany at the Cliffs of Moher and watched as our sister came back for a brief moment in time, remembering that she was worthy of love.

"That love miraculously came along in the form of a truly wonderful man—and right at the moment you were tested to see if you believed in that love, you failed. You failed miserably, Meg. Not only have you hurt your own heart, but you undoubtedly broke one of a man who so plainly and genuinely cares for you.

"What the fuck is wrong with you?"

"I don't know," I said, as the waterworks started up again. After this trip, I was certain I'd run out of tears for the next one hundred years.

"I—I just don't think it makes any sense to pursue something that inevitably has to end. How would we make it work? We live across the Atlantic Ocean from each other. It's complicated. Am I supposed to just believe that somehow things would work out?"

"Yes, damn it. It's called taking a risk—and it does

happen outside of your little advertising world. Maybe you are right—maybe it will blow up in your face and it won't last. But for crying out loud Meg, what if it can work out? What if what you've been looking for your entire life is right in front of your face?

"Are you really ready to just walk away from it? Do you think that we get so many chances at love that it's worth rolling the dice and hoping you'll find another perfect man close by in New York City? Seriously?"

I let the air fill with silence as I absorbed everything Marissa just said. I could only stare at this ring in my hand, remembering its significance and how it was bequeathed to me.

"Oh my God, what have I done?"

"Nothing that you can't fix," said Mia gently, lifting me up from the floor and handing me a tissue.

"How about we take this ring back to the hotel to keep it safe and then take one last go around Dublin. When we get back, you can call Kieran and work it all out. I'm thinking he will need the day to cool down, but I have no doubt he'd rather be with you than without you."

"I really hurt him, Mi. You should have seen the look on his face."

"Well, then it's up to you to bring the smile back. Fight for love, Meg. You deserve it."

"Thanks. I don't know what I would do without either of you." I embraced them before Marissa let out one of her perfectly timed cynical comments.

"You would make a complete mess of your life."

Back at the hotel, we decided to each freshen up before heading out for lunch in the fair city of Dublin. My mind was racing with how I would apologize to Kieran and ask for his forgiveness.

What a mess you've made this time, Rossi.

I took out the ring one last time for inspiration, noticing a note inside of the box. We must have missed it tucked inside the back corner while admiring the sparkly jewel at the bank. Seeing as it was a bit weathered itself, I carefully opened it up, curious about what it would say. I figured it was probably the legacy letter that Colleen mentioned came along with the inheritance.

As I read the words, a smile came over my face and I knew exactly what I needed to do. I protectively pocketed the tattered piece of paper, leaving the valuable ring locked safely back in the box and on the nightstand before meeting my sisters in the lobby. It was time to take a break from all this drama.

Lunch was outstanding. Mia had somehow managed to get us in to the 1592 Restaurant—a dining establishment not even open to the general public. I had to give it to her—she was craftier than I gave her credit for.

It was an adorable little place, more traditional in style than the city splendor that surrounded it. Knowing this could be the last fine dining experience of our trip, we decided that good old Granda Leigh would not be disappointed in our indulgence.

We each ordered something different so we could share plates, selecting from marinated chicken breasts, baked cod and sirloin steak, accompanied by mushroom risotto and buttered asparagus—and of course, a Bailey's Irish cheesecake to top it all off.

I decided to tuck my troubles away and just enjoy this time with my sisters. We chatted about the diary and the mystery, and they filled me in more about Clare Island.

We imagined what our trip to Italy would be like, teasing Mia about what mishaps she would drag us into on her journey.

As we were already on campus, we explored Trinity College, admiring all the history it held, from books and literary exhibitions to an ancient harp and beautifully manicured gardens.

"Mom would love this place," Mia mused, as we agreed.

So would Daddy, I thought. *What would he think of the disaster I've made of my life today?* I wondered.

Our tour coming to an end, we decided it would be best to pack up our stuff and head back to the west coast early. We only had two more days and with the ring in hand, we could spend the rest of our time just relaxing in our ancestral home.

The moment we arrived back at the hotel, our plans were thwarted. Seeing my door slightly open—forcibly so—I quietly tiptoed backwards so as to not be heard by an intruder, and then ran straight to the lobby to report the break-in. I didn't know if anyone was still in there, but I wasn't about to be one of those crazy suspense knuckleheads who tried to go inside and check it out by themselves.

Mia and Marissa met me in the hallway by my room as the hotel manager and security guards rushed from the elevator. They had already called the Dublin Garda, who were on the way. Stepping aside, we let the armed security guards enter first, to find no one inside. Waving us in, I gasped to see how wrecked my room was.

"Just like the O'Sullivan house was," I whispered.

"Sorry?" asked the guard.

"We were staying at our family home in Louisburgh

and had a similar break-in earlier this week. Everything was disheveled, but nothing was taken. Same here, except—"

I froze. The box! The lockbox was gone.

"Meg, what is it? What's missing?" prodded Mia.

"The ring. They took the ring."

"How could they take the ring? Didn't you lock it in the safe?" Marissa demanded.

"I wasn't thinking, I guess. I figured we were only going to be out for a little while and I had the privacy sign on the door so housekeeping would not come in, so I thought it would be fine right here by the bed."

"Can you describe this ring to us, miss? I'm also gonna be needing a formal statement," said the lead officer, who had just arrived. I went through the motions, explaining everything I knew, showing them the picture from Colleen that I happened to bring with me.

Mia and Marissa had their turn speaking with the Garda, noting that their rooms were undisturbed. We gave them our contact information and they said they would be in touch after reviewing the security footage and conducting their investigation.

When they were done in the room, they left us to gather our things so we could head back west. One of the guards remained outside of the door and planned to escort us to my sisters' rooms to retrieve their luggage, and then to the train station to ensure our continued safety.

All I could do was stand there in disbelief before starting to pack.

"I can't believe it. So, someone must have been after the ring the whole time. But who?" Mia asked.

"Beats me. Like Colleen said, not many people knew about it. I'm guessing we should do some digging into who might know about it within different extended family lines. So much for preserving its secret," I muttered.

"I'm so sorry you lost the ring, Meg. I hope they find it and put the jackass behind bars."

"It's okay, Mar. It's just a ring."

"How can you be so calm about this? Someone has broken into your space—twice—scared you half to death and stolen your inheritance worth over a half million dollars."

"Whoever was following me has finally gotten what he or she wanted. Now, maybe we'll be left alone in peace. Let them have it—there are more valuable things in this life than an old ring. We are safe and no one was hurt. I have everything I need in front of me."

"Not everything," Mia reminded me.

"Almost everything."

14

As expected, both Colleen and Kieran were waiting at the house upon our arrival—as were our favorite armed guards. Mia had forewarned me that she called Kieran to explain what happened and softened him up enough for him to join us.

Just seeing him set off rockets of different emotions, from fear and shame to pure joy and relief. He could barely look at me, I noticed. Colleen, oblivious to our tension, rushed over to us in mad worry.

"Oh my dears, I'm so glad you're not hurt! I feel terrible for my part in this. I shoulda told Leigh this would be too dangerous and to keep you out of it. Bound to be someone sniffin' around after a rich man's funeral, I told him, I did."

"It's okay, Colleen," I told her softly. "Everyone is safe now. They got what they wanted. Hopefully that's the end of it."

"Well, now that I know you are all safe here with the guards, I'd best be on my way," said Kieran.

I impulsively grabbed him by the arm. "Wait. Please."

He just turned and looked at me with a mix of anger and pain, driving a knife into my heart. Peering around at the other company, I used my eyes to plead them for a little privacy. Mia took the hint and escorted Marissa and Colleen to the bedrooms to unpack so we could have our space.

All I could do when we were alone was look at him with such regret. I stood there, all the words I rehearsed in my head gone. I just didn't know what to say.

"What do you want with me, Megan? I thought you said everything that needed to be said."

"I know you are angry, and you have every right to be. Can—can we sit down for a minute?" I motioned towards the sofa that held the memories of our passionate embraces. Begrudgingly, he followed my lead.

"I'm sorry, Kieran. I am really, really sorry. I was so scared, and I didn't know how to handle my feelings about leaving you and I just—I blew it."

"Blew what? It was just a fling, remember?" Ouch. I flinched like he had just hit me in the head with a ceramic vase. I deserved that.

"No, it wasn't. It's not. I've tried to fight it, but I can't. And I was wrong, so incredibly wrong, to act as if it was nothing—like *you* were nothing. Being with you is something I have never experienced in my entire life.

"I let myself fall into this abyss where I lost control of my emotions, let myself feel completely free—and when the reality hit that my time here was coming to an end, I went into default mode and hardened out of fear.

"I had to protect my heart. I'm so frightened of what I feel and the fact that I can't control it, that I can't for certain say that I know how it will all work out—it just paralyzed me."

We sat there speechless for a moment. He was softening, but I saw I still had some work to do. I could feel him demanding my vulnerability at all costs—at the cost of his love.

"It's not easy for me to be so open, Kieran. This is

new territory for me. I don't need to divulge my deepest sentiments in a client meeting or with a random lover. But with you, it's different. You make me feel so unbelievably loved and beautiful and accepted fully for who I am—all of me.

"I'm terrified of losing control of my life, of letting my heart take over and lead the way. But, I'm even more terrified of losing you."

Pausing, I took a deep breath. I moved my hand over his and instead of flinching, he took it in his, waiting for me to finish.

"I love you, Kieran. God help me, I am so completely and unreasonably in love with you. I know I have to stop being so cynical and trust myself and my heart for once in my life. I don't deserve a second chance after what I said to you, but I'm asking for one anyway. Can you ever forgive me?"

"I suppose so," he said with a slight smile. "But is this really what you want, Meg? Really, truly what you want? I need to know for certain. It's not easy for me to lend my heart out for the risk, either, you know."

"Yes. I want you. I want us. The second you walked out the door this morning I crumbled. I—I don't know if I can truly live without loving you. But I also don't know how it could work. I mean, truthfully, I don't know where to go from here."

"You're getting in your head again, *a ghrá*. We'll sort it out."

"You seem so confident about it. How can you be so sure? We live in two different countries, lead two different lifestyles. I try not to be in my head, but how could I not be?"

"Have a little faith. You're not the only one with

inheritance money, you know. I have plenty to use for a few trips to New York. We can make it work, but *a ghrá*, sometimes it takes a bit of effort. It's not always an easy road. But it's worth a try, isn't it?"

"If it means having you love me, it's worth more than just a try." With that, I reached over to tenderly kiss him. A kiss never felt so wonderful, because it meant that all was right with the world—our world.

Our full-on reconciliation was interrupted by the chuckling of a few recent eavesdroppers.

"I guess it's safe to come down now?" Marissa teased.

"It is," I laughed.

"Well done, you two. I'm glad you be back together and all, but can we get down to the business at hand? What are you be going to do about that ring of yours?" asked Colleen.

"Well—" I smiled sheepishly.

"What is it, Meg?" asked Mia.

"I actually have something to tell you." I paused for effect. "The ring wasn't stolen."

"What are you talking about? Of course it was—we were right there with you when you realized it was gone," stated Marissa, confused.

"Actually, that was a decoy ring. The original ring is hidden safely somewhere else. Here—read this." I took the folded note out from my pocket and handed it to Marissa to read out loud.

To the heir of this magnificent ring,

Though we do our best to preserve this family secret, many a greedy fool will try to gain possession of this treasure. To keep it safe, I have created this mock ring in its likeness. Let it be revealed as true; and then once safe, the faithful jewel can be found in the protection of Our Lady of St. Mary—at the very church down the road from the O'Sullivan family home.

Ye need only ask for the head priest, who has vowed to hold this secret in the confidence of this church until the rightful heir comes to claim it. There, ye shall find the legacy letter and the many blessings that accompany it. Honor and cherish this mighty band as I did and do right by your heritage in the name of love.

Yours, Lena O'Sullivan

"Wow," Mia said. "So, you knew this whole time that only a fake was stolen, and that the real one was here? No wonder why you were so cool when it all went down!"

"Why didn't you tell us?" asked Marissa, disconcerted.

"I thought it was best I told everyone at once. Besides, I didn't want any of the Garda to know until I had the real one in my possession and was out of the country.

"They can close the case or pursue it when we are gone; but for now, I didn't want anyone at all to overhear us or get wind of it and chance them finding the true ring. I liked knowing, at least for the moment, that we were all out of harm and wanted to keep it that way."

"Smart lass, she is, she is!" declared Colleen. "So, you'll be going to get it in the morning then, will you?"

"Yeah, it's been a long day. We can take off after breakfast and finish our journey here once and for all."

"Actually, I think Marissa and I should stay behind. I think you and Kieran should do this together—without us." Marissa returned her consent.

"But this is your inheritance and legacy as much as mine. We are in this together. I can't do this without you,"

I contested.

"Meg's right. I shouldn't even be here to begin with. This is your family journey. I shouldn't have any part in it, other than to just love on this one as much as I can before she leaves," Kieran argued.

"That's exactly why you *should* be the one to go with Meg. Look, we appreciate you thinking of us, but it isn't our place to be there. The heir of the ring should be joined by her love and read the legacy letter together. We can read it when you get back," Marissa added.

"Okay, then. Kieran, are you okay with this? Can you go with me in the morning?"

There was that warm dimpled smile I missed so much. "There's nothing I'd love better. But on one condition."

"What's that?"

"That at some point tomorrow, you come meet my mum before she cuts me head off."

"Deal," I laughed. "So, what do you all say we sit down and order in a nice quiet family dinner?"

"That sounds lovely," replied Mia.

"Actually," proposed Kieran, "I have a better idea."

A night at Gov's was exactly what the doctor ordered after another long day. It was the perfect way to lift our spirits, dining on a hearty meal, chatting with our new buddy Tuggs and other locals, and watching my beloved fall into his soul as he played his keyboard with the band.

It was nice to sit back and indulge in some small talk and laughter. Mia updated us on some humorous mini disasters Mom and Granny were having at home with juggling the kids' schedules and attitudes. Kieran and I talked about where I would bring him when he visited in a few weeks and prepared him for the investigative questioning he would undoubtedly receive from the rest of the family.

We also admired a new Celtic ring Marissa was wearing—a Claddagh of her own, which she claimed she purchased at a souvenir shop while we were paying for merchandise in another. We all agreed we had plenty of keepsakes racked up over two weeks that would fill one suitcase alone.

Not wanting to make my sisters or Colleen uncomfortable in the small house with thin walls, Kieran invited me to spend the night at his place instead. Bidding adieu to my approving sisters and cousin, off we went to his cottage.

It was hard to see the details in the dark, but it looked as sweet as I imagined it would be. His mum was already asleep in her room, thankfully on the first floor and far enough away from Kieran's upstairs bedroom for plenty of privacy. I never loved on a man with such heart and soul as I did that night.

In the morning, we were greeted by a tall, striking elderly woman with gray-black tendrils, familiar blue-green eyes and a delicate china doll face. I half expected his mother to be another little Irish bitty, but she was not the withered, sick old lady Kieran had led me to believe she was. She smiled at us coming down the stairs—a smile that quite clearly she handed down to her son.

"Well, I'll be! Is this the mysterious Miss Megan that has stolen me lad's heart?"

"It is," Kieran beamed proudly. "Morning, Mum." He went over to give her a peck, then brought me over to be formally introduced. She wrapped me in a big bear hug and I loved her instantly.

"I was just about to make breakfast. You hungry?"

"I can make breakfast, Mum. Why don't you sit down?"

"I'll have none of that, lad. You know I am perfectly capable of making breakfast."

Turning to me, she asked, "Is he this bossy with you too, lass? Thinks just because his mum hurt her hip a while back that she's incapable of living. I still have me arms, ya know."

I couldn't help but laugh as he shook his head. "I tried Mum, but Meg here has already set me straight on her being an independent woman and all."

"Well done," she said approvingly.

We enjoyed a simple family breakfast getting to know each other. I could tell that he got more than his smile from his mum—he had her innate kindness and generosity, along with her stubbornness. I loved witnessing their own little family dynamic and grew even fonder of him, seeing how much they adored and looked out for each other.

"Well, we best be going now, Mum."

"Where are you off to?"

"Meg has some family business to finish up this morning and then I thought we'd just head back to the O'Sullivan house and spend some time together before she flies home tomorrow."

"Oh, darn. I was just getting to enjoy your company and now you're going. Safe travels, lass," she said with an embrace. "You are welcome back here anytime, you know. Any time a'tall."

"Thank you. It was a pleasure meeting you. Say— would you like to come over for dinner? My sister is an outstanding cook and we would love for you to join us on our last night."

"That sounds lovely! It would be grand to take a night off meself and enjoy another's home cooking. Kieran darling, just give me a ring when you have the time and I'll get myself all ready. How delightful!"

In the truck, Kieran leaned over and gave me a long, hard kiss. "You just made my mum's whole life with that invitation, you know. She's quite fond of you, I can tell."

"I'm fond of her, too. You made her seem like some elderly old woman who could barely walk. She seems perfectly healthy to me."

"Ay that she is, I suppose. I guess I need to work on my overprotective skills," he relented. "Oh—wait a minute. I almost forgot something."

He jumped out of the truck and ran back into the house for a moment.

"What's wrong?" I asked when he came back winded.

"Never you mind. Are you ready to go get that ring?"

"Let's do it!"

We agreed that we would park his truck at the house, go inside to say a quick morning hello and change my clothes, and then take a walk down to the church. It had been raining all night and the overcast sky threatened to open up again, but he assured me that we would be fine.

I told my sisters and cousin I had invited Mrs. MacGovern to dinner, which pleased Colleen immensely. I was going to miss our bubbly old cousin, but we already agreed to monthly video calls to stay in touch.

While my sisters began to pack, Colleen offered to gather up the remaining old photos and journal to take home with us, along with a few other trinkets from the house that she was happy to part with.

The plan when we got back to the house was to enjoy the afternoon and evening quietly as a family before our flight first thing in the morning. It was bittersweet to see our trip come to an end, saying goodbye to the wonderful people we met, but we were ready to go home.

Boy, did we have some stories to share!

But first, I had a mission to complete. With Kieran's hand in mine, we set off for Our Lady of St. Mary's to claim the genuine *Legacy of Love Claddagh* ring.

The inside of the church was just as picturesque as the outside. Old, refurbished wooden pews lined the small room leading the way up to the altar, which was adorned with white and gold fabric, tall gold candelabras and fresh white floral arrangements on each side.

Above the altar in honor of the church was an intricate sculpture of the Mother Mary built into the wall, hands spread out as if blessing the congregation. The stained glass windows that lined the side of the wall depicted various religious symbols and stories, wrought with detail and sacred meaning.

Although I was not much of a churchgoer, I couldn't help but find myself enamored with the tiny cathedral. From behind a starch white curtain came an elderly priest, perhaps well into his eighties, donning a pristine white and gold robe and holding a Bible to his heart.

"Ah, welcome, my children. May I help you?"

"Good morning, Father. I am looking for the Head Priest of this church."

"That would be me. I'm Father Joyce." We bowed in his presence.

"It's nice to meet you, Father Joyce. My name is Megan Rossi. I am Colleen O'Sullivan's cousin and descendant of Cian and Alessia O'Sullivan. Have you heard of us by any chance?"

"I have indeed. I have been waiting for you, Ms. Rossi. I believe I have something precious of yours in the back here. Please wait right here a moment."

"Wait," I stopped him. "Don't you need some kind of identification or proof of who I am or something?"

He had a somewhat toothless, yet lovable grin. "My child, I would know a daughter of the O'Sullivan line anywhere. You look just like old Cian from the photos I've seen. Your family is legend in this town. There be no doubt in my mind that you are the rightful heir."

Within minutes, he was back with an absolutely beautiful, dark Kelly green Fabergé egg with an intricately designed trim of golden Celtic knots. He presented it to me, gesturing for me to open it in his company. Inside was a stunning statuette of a green and gold Claddagh symbol, and within the empty space of the Claddagh heart were the tied strings of a small black felt bag.

My heart pounding, I opened the bag to reveal the *Legacy of Love Claddagh* ring—its brilliance blinding like the sun. The decoy had nothing on the original. Unlike the fake version, this band happened to be a perfect fit as I slid it onto my right ring finger to embrace it with all its glory.

Father Joyce then motioned to a small latch under the stand of the egg, which when opened, revealed an ancient piece of parchment paper.

"The legacy letter," I deduced. I delicately opened it up, making sure to preserve its integrity and protect it from ripping. I looked up at Father Joyce and thanked him for watching over our family legacy.

"It has been an honor, Miss Megan. Would you mind doing an old man a favor, though?"

"Of course. What is it?"

"This egg has been under the church's protection for over fifty years—thirty under my sole care. It would warm my heart if I could share in the reading of the legend. I vow to never speak of it to another soul. I should know better than to be intrigued by worldly possessions such as these, but I can't help but to wonder about the story behind it all."

"Of course, Father. I can think of no better place than to read it right here." Beaming like a little boy on Christmas morning, the priest took his place on the bench to my left, while Kieran joined me on my right.

THE LEGEND OF THE LEGACY OF LOVE CLADDAGH

In the year of 1682, a noble king, King Padraig II, asked young silversmith Duncan McGuinness to fashion him a unique ring intended for his new bride. He had given the lad a rare green diamond, the richest jewel in all the land.

When young Duncan asked the name of the king's intended so that he may bring her spirit into his creation, he was heartbroken to learn it was his own Maeve Flanagan.

Although from different upbringings—Maeve's of nobility and Duncan's of simple silversmiths—the two younglings had a fondness for each other as children, sneaking off to play in the woods and spend days by the creek.

As they grew older, fondness turned to love, and they planned to run away so they could be together. But as Duncan found out that very day, Sir Flanagan had promised his daughter Maeve to the king and that ended all dreams of being together.

Woefully broken hearted, Duncan decided to leave his Maeve

one last piece of himself to remember their love. So, being in his truest of heart, he forged the ring with the green diamond in the symbol of the Claddagh, created a band in the likeness of the trinity knot and added a drop of his blood to the branding fire as it closed the hands around the heart.

The king was quite pleased with the one-of-a-kind ring and when presented to his almost bride, it was said she could feel the presence of love within the exquisite band. She asked to be taken to its maker to thank him for his gifted work, unbeknownst to either that the silversmith was indeed her truest love.

When she found out it was Duncan, and he acknowledged that it was his blood within the ring he designed for her out of his own love, she agreed to follow him into their special woods for a final moment together before accepting her fate as future queen. There, they made love for the first and only time, with Maeve giving him the gift of her innocence and the ring symbolically set firm upon her left hand.

After they were joined in sacred love, the Goddess Danu came upon them and blessed their union and the ring forevermore.

Angered that fate was to keep them apart, Maeve declared that she would no longer wear the ring if she was not with her true love, for it would break its spell. She henceforth lied to the king about the ring being stolen and hid it where it could never be found by the kingsmen: in the nook of the tree where the lovers joined.

Shortly thereafter, on the eve of their wedding, Maeve found herself to be with Duncan's child. The king was none too pleased to find out he was betrayed and that his bride was not his virgin to take.

But fearing ridicule of his people and the shame if the truth were told, he forced Maeve to claim the child as his and they wed before delivering the happy news to the kingdom. The king then had Duncan hunted down and killed, ending the love affair forever.

Crushed, she gave her body to the king to do what he wished with it, knowing she would never find joy again—until her love child, Aine, was born.

She went on to have other children with the king, proper male heirs to his pleasure. When the king died and the first son took over, the queen Maeve was then free to disclose the truth to her Aine alone, along with the ring and its legend—with the promise that only her rightful heirs who mirror the value of her heart and share the truest of loves would know the truth and the blessing of this treasure.

Maeve then went back to the forest where she and Duncan made love and took her own life to finally be with her beloved, the ring once again upon her finger. As Aine returned to that very spot to honor her parents, it is said that they both appeared over their daughter, ring now on her finger, and sanctified the magical love that it possessed.

It did eventually bring Aine great true love, and so she carefully dictated this story and passed on the secret blessing to her firstborn daughter, Fiona. And it is I, Fiona, who have written this tale of love for my heirs to witness.

May he or she who is blessed to carry on the legacy of love live on in consecrated bliss with their beloved, as my mother, Aine, and her daughters after did. For there be no truer jewel of love than the one forged with the blood of a sacred lover, consecrated *by the goddesses and blessed by the original paramours in death's reunion.*

Go gcuire Dia an t-ádh ort.

"That was a mighty beautiful story. Thank you for sharing that with me, child. Allow me before you part to bestow a blessing upon you."

He brought me up to the altar, dipped his fingers in holy water, granted me a special blessing of devotion and affirmed the sacred powers of the ring would carry out its loving intention in the name of God. I was touched by the gesture, already feeling stronger in love than before I walked in.

We thanked him for his help and the blessing. Knowing how conspicuous carrying and packing such a valuable Fabergé egg would be, we asked him to keep it in the church's possession to help preserve the protection of the ring.

Stepping out of the church, I felt an enormous sense of relief. Finally, I had my family heirloom safely in my possession, the immediate danger suspended by a clever faux ring. I now had a critical piece of knowledge not only about my ancestors, but also about the heritage behind this extraordinary jewel.

But what relieved me most was that my heart had finally opened to love, and he was standing here, right beside me, and he wasn't a dream. I didn't need Father Joyce's blessing—I was already blessed. I turned and smiled adoringly at my own beloved, taking his hand in mine so that we could walk back home united.

"Meg, wait a minute. I have something for you." Curious, I followed his lead as he took me over to the ruins—to that sacred altar where lovers used to marry.

"What is it?" He reached into his pocket and pulled out a gorgeous pendant, surprisingly a replica design of the *Legacy of Love Claddagh* ring—right down to the green heart in its center.

"A few days ago, when I was running some errands for Mum, I took a picture of your ring down to my jeweler friend and asked if he could forge a matching pendant with an emerald. Don't worry though, *a ghrá*; I told him that I found this random photograph on the internet—he was none the wiser about its origin."

"It's the most beautiful and thoughtful gift anyone has ever given me. Thank you."

"Without knowing the content of that letter, I had this forged under the same kind of love—except for my blood, of course. Be it a symbol of how I feel about you, to remind you that you are my own one-of-a-kind jewel, even when we are apart.

"I love you, *mo shíorghrá*. I don't know where the road will be taking us, but I hope it takes us together. As the proverb goes: 'The future is not set; there is no fate but what we make for ourselves.'"

I decided to accept his unconditional love with a proverb of my own remembrance. "'You for me and I for thee and never another. Your face turned to mine and away from all others.'"

Then right there, upon the sacred ruins, we pledged our eternal love and sealed it with a kiss. Our life together had just begun—there was no knowing where it would lead, but for once in my life, I was going to follow my heart.

O'Sullivan Family Line

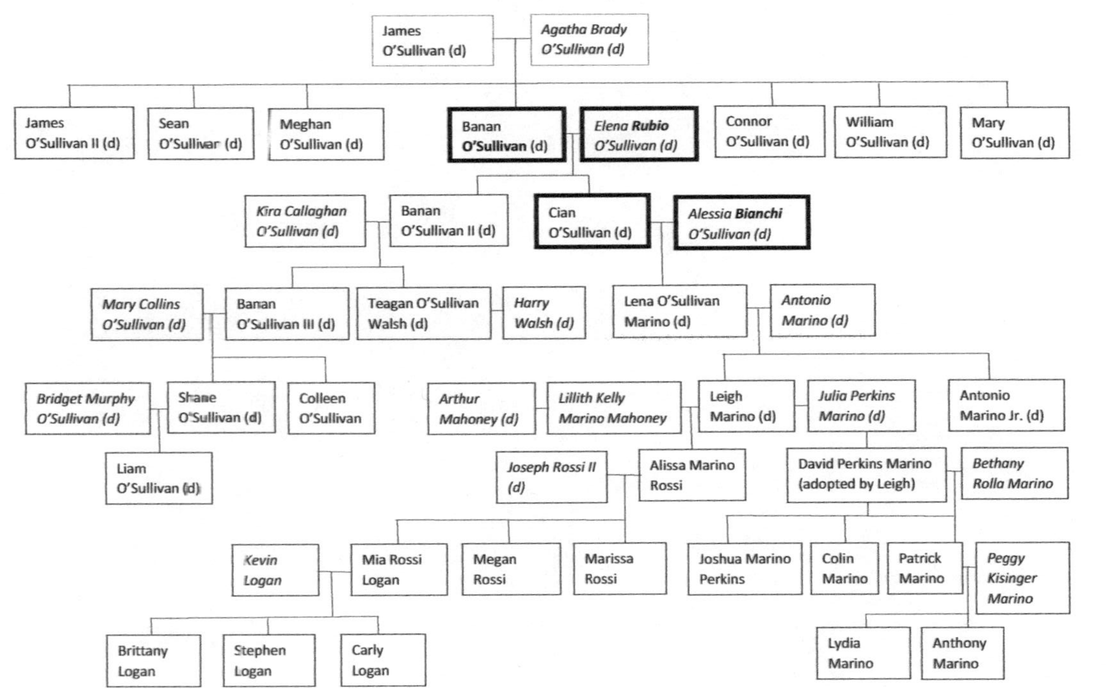

A Tuscan Treasure

BOOK TWO OF THE LOST HERITAGE TRILOGY

The journey continues. Can Mia find the strength to fight back against all odds?

Walking in on her husband in bed with a 20-year-old was the last thing Mia Logan expected when she arrived home from a wonderful sister trip in Ireland. Now a single mom with a broken heart and low self-esteem, she must pick up the pieces of her life and move on. Her unrelenting depression and the looming danger of a committed stalker almost keep the peacemaking middle sister from retrieving her inherited jewelry box in the beautiful city of Florence, Italy. Determined to fight back and regain her life, she ultimately makes the voyage that opens countless doors—to her long-forgotten dreams, to reignited passion and to her heart. Thrust into an unforeseen romance with the charming Francesco Marchesi, her cousin Maria's trusted lawyer, Mia faces her greatest challenge yet: learning to love herself exactly as she is.

COMING MAY 2020